Terror at High Tide

Joe had to concentrate hard to keep his balance while he climbed aboard the sailboard. Finally he was up. Grasping the handle on the sail, he steadied the craft against the brisk wind as he glided out to sea. Squinting against the sunlight and the saltwater spray as he zoomed along, Joe couldn't see the boat he was trying to follow.

Suddenly Joe heard a ripping sound. Glancing up, he saw the sail hanging in shreds above his head. Then the sail started to swing around wildly. Joe clung to the handle, struggling to keep his balance.

The sail tipped toward the ocean, smacking Joe into a wave. As he plunged into the water, the current swept the windsurfer out of his reach.

Joe began to swim for shore, but the harder he swam, the farther away from shore he seemed to go.

I'm caught in a riptide, he realized—and the current is sending me out to sea. I've got to get out of here fast—or I'll drown!

The Hardy Boys
Mystery Stories

Available from MINSTREL Books

THE HARDY BOYS®

145

TERROR AT HIGH TIDE

FRANKLIN W. DIXON

A MINSTREL® BOOK

Published by POCKET BOOKS
New York   London   Toronto   Sydney   Tokyo   Singapore

A MINSTREL PAPERBACK Original

A Minstrel Book published by
POCKET BOOKS, a division of Simon & Schuster Inc.
1230 Avenue of the Americas, New York, NY 10020

Copyright © 1997 by Simon & Schuster Inc.

Front cover illustration by John Youssi

Produced by Mega-Books, Inc.

All rights reserved, including the right to reproduce
this book or portions thereof in any form whatsoever.
For information address Pocket Books, 1230 Avenue
of the Americas, New York, NY 10020

ISBN: 0-671-00057-8

First Minstrel Books printing August 1997

10 9 8 7 6 5 4 3 2

THE HARDY BOYS MYSTERY STORIES is a trademark
of Simon & Schuster Inc.

THE HARDY BOYS, A MINSTREL BOOK and colophon
are registered trademarks of Simon & Schuster Inc.

Printed in the U.S.A.

Contents

TERROR AT
HIGH TIDE

1 Washed Ashore

"Surf's up," Frank Hardy said to his younger brother, Joe. "Those waves are awesome. Ready to catch a few?"

"I'm game if you are," Joe replied, grabbing his surfboard and heading out toward the turbulent sea. "Besides, I didn't come all the way from Bayport to Nantucket just to sunbathe."

Frank pushed his dark hair out of his eyes, looked out at the sparkling ocean, and chuckled. He should have known that Joe would want to plunge in the second they arrived at the beach, even though the surf was still heavy from a storm the day before.

Frank plopped his surfboard into the foamy

water, eased himself onto it, then paddled out to sea behind Joe.

"Yikes!" Joe cried as a mountain of water loomed up, blotting out the turquoise-colored sky. "That wave's a monster. Let's ride it."

"We either ride it or get creamed by it!" Frank shouted. He paddled hard toward the wave, making sure to keep a safe distance from Joe. The wave looked powerful enough to break a surfboard, Frank thought—he hated to think what it would do to *him* if he didn't reach it in time.

Catching a glimpse of Joe's wet blond head twenty feet away, Frank gritted his teeth. Joe looked like a tiny speck in the hollow of the giant wave. As the wave swelled higher, Frank could see Joe position his board in the middle, planting his feet firmly on it. He rose to a crouching position, holding his arms out for balance. Then he started to glide smoothly along. Way to go, Joe, Frank thought as the wave crested.

Frank hoped he could make it to the wave before it broke. He felt his biceps strain as he used every ounce of his strength to paddle. If he didn't get to the wave at just the right moment, he'd be in for a total wipeout.

Frank watched the wave make a final heave toward the sky, then begin to spill over. All he could see was a wall of dark water threatening to crash over him.

In a split second Frank reached the monster

wave as it broke. He brought his board around and hopped up. The wave was like a wild animal, doing its best to hurl him off, and Frank fought to keep just ahead of the danger zone.

"Cowabunga!" he shouted as he zipped along. Like a writhing sea snake, the wave tossed its way to shore, finally depositing Frank close to where Joe was standing in knee-deep water.

"I couldn't have done it better myself," Joe said as Frank zoomed up. "For a moment, though, I thought you were shark food, for sure."

Frank jumped off his surfboard and slapped Joe five. "You and me both," Frank admitted. "But somehow I got lucky. What do you say we take a beach break after that one? Callie and Alicia brought us some sodas."

Joe nodded. "Sounds great."

With surfboards in hand, the Hardys waded to shore, then headed across a strip of hot yellow sand to a colorfully striped beach umbrella. Frank's girlfriend, blond-haired Callie Shaw, looked up and waved at the Hardys as they approached while her friend, Alicia Geovanis, bent over a cooler, her red shoulder-length curls cascading down around her face.

"Hey, guys, that was some wave," Callie said, a mixture of concern and wonder in her voice. "I'm glad you made it to shore."

"Bet you could use an energy boost," Alicia

said, handing Frank and Joe each a soda. She smiled up at them, the skin on her freckled nose crinkling while she squinted into the sun.

As Frank and Joe sat down, Callie glanced at her watch. "I've got to get back to work by two o'clock," she said. "I promised the *Island News* I'd write up a story for tomorrow's paper."

"More hot news?" Joe said in a mock-serious tone. "You've already covered that big cat rescue from the rock at high tide."

Callie laughed. "I know, I know—and the pancake breakfast at the fire department. I admit I'm running low on ideas. I mean, being a summer intern at the newspaper here is great—but not much happens on Nantucket."

"That's the whole point," Alicia said. "It's peaceful and beautiful. People come here to relax—"

"Relax?" Callie cut in, her brown eyes twinkling. "Frank and Joe will change all that. They claim they're here for a week to visit me, but sooner or later they'll be solving some mystery that would completely baffle anyone else."

Frank and Joe were a formidable duo when it came to detective work.

"Thanks, Callie. We owe a lot to our dad," Frank said modestly, referring to Fenton Hardy, a private detective in Bayport, New York.

Joe nodded. "He's been a real inspiration."

After a brief pause Joe gave Frank a playful punch on the arm. "Finish your soda, bro. We've got some surfing to do."

"What!" Callie groaned. "Not again."

"I'm with you," Frank said as he got to his feet. He thanked the girls for the soda, then picked up his surfboard. When he lifted it, a swarm of flies rose from a clump of rotting seaweed a few feet away, revealing a thin red crescent at the seaweed's edge. Frank did a double take.

Frank put down his surfboard and squatted to get a better look. He wrinkled his nose. There was a smell of decay in the air—from the seaweed, he figured.

Gingerly Frank lifted the seaweed. Underneath, a red rubbery-looking object lay partly buried in the sand. Picking it up, Frank saw that it was a deflated balloon with white letters on it that spelled *Ebony Pearl.*

Wow, Frank thought—the *Ebony Pearl* was a famous shipwreck. He remembered reading that the ship had sunk off the shoals of Nantucket— an island off the coast of Cape Cod, Massachusetts—in 1957. Could this balloon have just washed up on shore, he wondered— forty years after the ship went down?

"Hey, Joe!" he called, gesturing to his brother, who was already setting his surfboard on the water. "Come here."

While Joe jogged up the beach, Frank walked over to the girls. "Look what I just found," he said, kneeling to show them the balloon.

Alicia's sunburned face turned pale. "I can't believe it," she whispered.

Joe let out a low whistle as he examined it. "Could this be for real?" he said. As he spoke, a wave streamed up the sand toward them and wet the edge of their beach blanket.

"The tide's coming in," Callie said. "With these waves, we'll be soaked in a second. Let's get out of here."

"Come on up to my house," Alicia offered. "We can look at the balloon there."

After handing the balloon back to Frank, Joe grabbed the surfboards and a backpack full of dry clothes, while Frank helped Callie with the umbrella and cooler. Then Frank, Joe, and Callie followed Alicia up a narrow path between the dunes. A short flight of wooden stairs led up to a gray shingled Cape Cod cottage that sat on a bluff above the ocean.

"Come on in, guys," Alicia said as she opened the door. They all stepped into a comfortable living room with wicker furniture, straw rugs— and sand on the floor. Magazines and books were strewn around the sofa, and two unwashed coffee cups sat on a nearby table.

"Sorry about the mess," Alicia said as she

began to clear off the sofa. "My dad has been busy at work, and I'm not much of a housekeeper. If my mom were still alive, she'd have this place shipshape."

"No problem," Joe said as he sat down on the sofa next to the others. "Believe me, housework is the last thing on my mind, too."

"What *is* on our minds," Frank said, tossing the balloon into the center of the coffee table, "is the *Ebony Pearl.* Your dad must know a lot about it. Wasn't it some kind of luxury liner, like the *Titanic?*"

Earlier, Alicia had explained to the Hardys that her father, George Geovanis, was an expert on shipwrecks. Alicia and her father had moved to Nantucket two months earlier. Her father was the new curator of the Nantucket Shipping Museum.

Holding the balloon, Alicia studied it thoughtfully. "The *Ebony Pearl* was a small luxury cruise ship with about four hundred passengers," she began, "nowhere near as large as the *Titanic.* It was on its way from Florida to Maine when it sank, and almost half the passengers drowned." She stopped, then frowned. Frank had a feeling there was more to her story.

"One of those who drowned was my grandfather, my father's dad," she finally said. "There wasn't enough time to lower all the lifeboats, and my grandmother and my dad barely made it."

"Your dad was on the *Ebony Pearl?*" Frank asked. "He must have been just a kid then."

"He was only ten years old," Alicia said softly. "The accident made a lasting impression on him. And my grandmother never got over my grandfather's death."

"What caused the accident?" Joe asked. "It must have been something big for there not to have been time to get all the lifeboats down."

"Something exploded," Alicia said. "They think it was the boiler. It happened in the middle of a dinner to honor the captain."

"Could we show this balloon to your dad?" Frank asked Alicia. "Would he be able to tell us if it's real?"

"Absolutely," Alicia replied. "He'll be extremely interested in it. It was his experience as a kid on the *Ebony Pearl* that made him so fascinated by shipwrecks."

She rose from the sofa. "Let's change first, though," she said, tossing Frank the pack full of clothes. "We can't wear bathing suits into the museum."

Thirty minutes later Frank, Joe, Callie, and Alicia climbed out of Alicia's red convertible Jeep outside the Nantucket Shipping Museum in the center of the historic old town. Frank and Joe knew that Nantucket had been a world-famous whaling port before the Civil War. These days vacationers flocked to the island for its good beaches and water sports, its seafood, and its rich maritime history.

Alicia led the way inside the museum, ushering her friends past the ticket taker, who gave them a friendly nod.

As they passed through the large airy main room of the museum, Frank and Joe saw ship models and artifacts of every kind, from models of Spanish galleons to paintings of Nantucket whaling ships and photographs of World War II battleships. There was even an authentic skull-and-crossbones flag from a pirate ship.

"Hey, look at that octopus," Joe said as they walked up a flight of stairs leading to a balcony level. Hanging from the ceiling were several types of stuffed sea creatures, including sharks, starfish, and a twelve-foot-long octopus.

"I wouldn't want that thing hugging me," Frank joked.

"Check this out," Joe said, once they had reached the top.

"It's the *Lusitania*," Frank said, reading from a placard next to a ship model, "the British ocean liner sunk by a German submarine in World War One."

"This entire front mezzanine displays

twentieth-century ocean liner shipwrecks—my father's special interest," Alicia said with a sweep of her hand. Next to the *Lusitania*, models of the *Titanic*, the *Andrea Doria*, and the *Ebony Pearl* sat out on exhibit stands. Artifacts from these ships, such as ashtrays, cutlery, champagne bottles, and jewels, were displayed in glass cases.

"It's hard to believe that all this stuff was once part of glamorous ocean liners," Callie said, shaking her head, "and then they all sank."

"Here's my dad's office," Alicia said. She knocked on a door just past the shipwreck exhibit. A placard outside read George Geovanis, Curator.

A middle-aged dark-haired man opened the door. When he saw Alicia, his intense brown eyes lit up. "Hi, dear," he said, giving his daughter a hug. "And hello, Callie."

After Callie and Geovanis exchanged greetings, Callie introduced him to Frank and Joe.

"Welcome to the shipping museum," Geovanis said, smiling warmly at the Hardys. He ushered everyone into his office, which was filled with books and manuscripts. A computer sat on a desk by a far window, along with various shipping knickknacks, including a dangerous-looking four-foot harpoon laid out on wooden blocks across the front of the desk. "What brings you all in here on such a good beach day?" he asked them.

Frank pulled the balloon from his pocket and handed it to Geovanis. "We wondered if you would mind taking a look at this, Mr. Geovanis. I found it near your house, washed up on the sand. Is there any way you could tell us whether it's really from the *Ebony Pearl*?"

"The *Ebony Pearl*, huh?" Geovanis said, peering at the balloon. "If it is real, this would be quite a find."

Geovanis knitted his brows as he examined the balloon under a magnifying glass. "The rubber is thicker than it is on balloons nowadays," he told them. "And there are cracks in the rubber which would fit with its being in sea water for so long. I'm quite sure it's authentic."

Frank noticed a small, sandy-haired man with wire-rimmed glasses standing in the doorway. He was listening to their conversation with a smug expression on his face. How long has that guy been there? Frank wondered. And who is he?

"Could I keep this for the museum?" Geovanis was saying, looking hopefully at Frank.

The sandy-haired man rushed into the room. "Let me see that!" he snapped, grabbing the balloon. He studied it for a moment, then looked up. "You're wrong, Geovanis!" he shouted, throwing the balloon onto the desk. "This balloon was not submerged in water for forty years.

11

This is a hoax—and you should know better if you value your job."

The man lifted the harpoon from the desk and waved it angrily, its razor-sharp point glinting in the fluorescent light. Then he stood poised, as if he was going to hurl it like a javelin—right at Mr. Geovanis!

2 Eight-Legged Enemy

Joe made a lunge for the man, but before he could grab him, the man lowered the harpoon, his arm shaking as he struggled to contain his anger.

"Roberto," Mr. Geovanis said sternly, his face pale. "You may not like it, but I am your boss now. And if you ever threaten me like that again, I will fire you and then I'll notify the police. Take this as my last warning."

"I'm sorry," the man said, placing the harpoon back on its wooden props. He looked awkwardly around at the group. "I won't forget myself like that again. But it's my duty to tell the truth. This balloon is not authentic."

"You may disagree with me," Mr. Geovanis

said, "and I'll consider your opinion. But I will draw my own conclusion about the balloon."

"*Consider* my opinion!" the man said hotly. "I'm sick of your condescending attitude! If you claim that this balloon is authentic, I'll deny it publicly—through the newspapers if need be." He turned on his heel and marched out of the room.

Joe was the first to break the stunned silence. "Who is that guy and what is his problem?" he asked Alicia's father.

"He's the assistant curator here, Roberto Scarlatti," Mr. Geovanis explained, taking a handkerchief from his pocket to wipe his brow. "And he's had a chip on his shoulder about me ever since I was hired."

"He's jealous of Dad," Alicia told them. She moved to the desk and gave her father a comforting hug. "And he's made working here a nightmare for him. Scarlatti just couldn't take it that Dad got the job as curator."

"You see," Mr. Geovanis went on, looking at Callie and the Hardys, "Roberto's worked at the museum for over fifteen years. He thinks he deserved the promotion, but instead the job went to me, an island newcomer."

"Why didn't he get the promotion?" Frank asked, his dark eyes looking curious.

"Well," Mr. Geovanis said slowly, "Roberto's

knowledge of shipping *is* impressive, but as you can see, his personality is explosive. A curator has to be good at public relations and fund-raising. That means knowing how to be friendly and diplomatic. Roberto doesn't exactly fit the job description."

That's the understatement of the year, Joe thought, exchanging glances with Frank. He could tell that his brother agreed with him that Roberto Scarlatti was one weird dude.

"Roberto is always looking for ways to discredit me," Mr. Geovanis said, "but he's never had an outburst like this before." He bit his lip, looking worried. "In any case, I know my job is secure no matter what mischief Roberto cooks up. I've done a lot for the museum in the short time since I've been here—organizing some interesting exhibits and drawing in more people."

"Is there any chance that Scarlatti could be right about the balloon?" Joe asked.

Mr. Geovanis shrugged. "I've never been wrong so far, but there's always a first time."

"Why would the balloon wash up now, after forty years under the sea?" Frank asked.

Mr. Geovanis frowned. "I don't know," he admitted after a pause. "Maybe it had been caught underneath something, and with the shifting of the ocean floor over the years, it was finally dislodged."

"Callie," Joe teased, "you've got your hot story

now—the whole island will be interested in a balloon from the *Ebony Pearl*."

"That's exactly what I've been thinking, Joe," Callie said. "I'm off to the *Island News* right now so I can write up my story before the paper goes to press." She chuckled. "But I don't think I'll include Mr. Scarlatti's outburst—that's too much excitement, even for me."

Joe shot Frank a challenging look. "Speaking of excitement, why don't we head back to the beach to ride a few more waves?"

"You guys can borrow my Jeep," Alicia said, handing Joe the keys. "I'd like to do some shopping in town, and Dad can give me a ride home later."

Frank and Joe thanked Alicia and said goodbye to Mr. Geovanis. Then Callie, Frank, and Joe headed out the door. "What's your gut feeling about the balloon, Frank?" Joe asked in a low voice as they stepped out of the museum. "Do you think Mr. Geovanis is right about it?"

"Probably," Frank answered. "He's the expert. Though his own experience with the shipwreck might sway him about the balloon."

"What do you mean?" Callie asked.

Frank shrugged. "It's just that Mr. Geovanis might *want* the balloon to be real—to connect him again to his father."

"So he might overlook evidence that the balloon's not really from the *Ebony Pearl?*" Joe asked.

"Not on purpose," Frank replied. "I hope Mr. Geovanis is right—I wouldn't want that slime Scarlatti to have the last laugh."

Joe frowned. "That guy is the human equivalent of Mount Vesuvius. He could erupt at any time. I don't see how Mr. Geovanis can work with him."

"I wonder what Scarlatti's reaction will be tomorrow after he reads about the balloon in the newspaper," Callie mused, shooting Frank a wry grin. "I wouldn't want to be within earshot of the guy."

After firming up plans to meet Callie for breakfast the next morning, Frank and Joe waved goodbye to her and climbed into Alicia's Jeep. Then they headed back to the beach to spend the rest of the afternoon surfing.

"Check out this headline, Joe," Frank said the next morning as he held up the front page of the *Island News.* He and Joe were standing inside the Hub, a book and newspaper shop on Main Street.

Glancing over Frank's shoulder, Joe read, "'Shipwrecked Balloon Washes Ashore!' I'm impressed. Callie's story is front-page news."

"The *Ebony Pearl?*" an elderly man in tennis whites said. "What about it?"

"You'll have to buy the *Island News* to find out, Mr. Lewis," the man behind the counter told him. "But you'd better hurry—I'm running low. The whole town wants to read about it."

As Mr. Lewis reached behind Joe for a newspaper, Joe shot Frank a wide grin. "How does it feel to be famous, Frank?" he asked in a low voice. "Callie's article mentions you by name. It says, 'The amazing discovery was made by Frank Hardy of Bayport, New York, at about three o'clock yesterday afternoon.'"

"Shhh," Frank said, putting on a pair of sunglasses. "I don't want to be recognized."

Joe rolled his eyes. "I'll do my best to shield you from the paparazzi."

After paying for their newspaper, Frank and Joe headed across the street to the Muffin Café, where they were planning to meet Callie for breakfast.

"Hi, guys," Callie called from the doorway. "I've saved us a table in the back garden," she said, leading the way through the restaurant.

"Sorry we're late," Frank said as they sat down at their table. "But we had to stop to buy a copy of the *Island News*. We didn't want to miss the lead story." He tossed the newspaper onto the table.

Callie's face lit up. "Did you read the story?

18

What did you think? Does it seem more exciting than the pancake breakfast?"

"Slow down," Frank said, grinning. "One question at a time. Yes, I read the story. And yes, I think it's great. But no, it's not as exciting as the pancake breakfast."

Callie laughed, then made a face at Frank. "Give me a break, will you?"

As they looked at their menus, Joe overheard some people at the next table talking about the *Ebony Pearl.* No doubt about it, he thought, Callie's story is the talk of the island.

Joe noticed Roberto Scarlatti sitting alone at a table nearby. He was drinking coffee and reading a copy of the *Island News,* an angry scowl on his face. As Joe nudged Frank and Callie, Scarlatti threw the paper down on an empty chair. "Rubbish," he muttered in disgust. Then he plunked down some change on his table and got up to leave.

"Mr. Scarlatti," Joe said, rising quickly from his chair. "I'm Joe Hardy. I met you yesterday at the museum."

"Yes?" Scarlatti said, looking at Joe coolly. Joe wasn't sure if Scarlatti remembered him.

"I noticed you reading the newspaper, and I wondered what you thought of the lead story," Joe said.

Scarlatti frowned—like a thundercloud about to explode, Joe thought. He hoped the guy wouldn't blow his cool right there in the restaurant.

"The article is absurd," Scarlatti spat out. "It reported what that imbecile George Geovanis said, no questions asked. I'm going to the *Island News* right now to set the record straight. I'll make them publish *my* story tomorrow."

Onlookers at nearby tables glanced at Scarlatti with curiosity as he stormed out of the café.

"Hmm," Callie said, her brown eyes looking worried. "I hope I won't have to write up *that* story. It would make a terrific article, but Scarlatti sure has a short fuse. He might blow up during the interview."

"Let's order," Frank said, "so we can get going. How about a little kayaking after breakfast, Joe?"

"Sounds good to me," Joe replied as he studied the menu. "I don't know how you can call this breakfast, though. All I see here is muffins. Where are the steak and eggs? Or at least one measly little hot dog?"

"For breakfast?" Callie said with a smile. "Yuck." She glanced at her watch. "I've got to be at work soon, but why don't we meet at the Atlantic Café for dinner? There is something on that menu for everyone—even Joe," she added with a mischievous grin.

* * *

At eleven o'clock that evening Frank, Joe, Callie, and Alicia were walking down South Beach Street, eating ice-cream cones. Frank and Joe carried skateboards under their arms, and Callie and Alicia wheeled bicycles.

"Let's see if *you* can skateboard and eat ice cream at the same time," Joe said.

"Just because you dropped your cone and had to get a new one . . ." Frank said with a chuckle. "But, okay, I'll give it a try."

Frank put down his board, then pushed off, and zoomed half a block down the street while skillfully maneuvering around a couple of pedestrians. As he flipped to a stop, he took a bite of his cone.

"Dumb luck," Joe muttered as he caught up with Frank.

Frank, Joe, Callie, and Alicia had eaten a huge seafood dinner and then seen a movie. While they were getting ice cream, Alicia had offered to give them a private tour of the shipping museum as the perfect way to cap off the evening.

Joe wondered why Alicia had been so quiet all evening—not at all like her usual bubbly self. When she and Callie caught up with the Hardys, Joe asked her what was wrong.

"I'm worried about my dad," Alicia explained. "He's been preoccupied ever since this morning."

"What happened this morning?" Joe asked.

"That worm Scarlatti wrote a nasty rebuttal to Callie's article," Alicia said. "He said that Dad was totally uninformed about the balloon. Then he went over to the paper to get them to publish it."

"I know," Callie said. "A reporter was working on it for tomorrow's paper."

Alicia sighed. "Dad's at a dinner party right now for a guy named Harrison Cartwright, who's campaigning to be a selectman of the town. A lot of Dad's friends are there. I hope the party will cheer him up."

"Selectman? What's that?" Joe asked her, hoping to take Alicia's mind off her worries.

"Nantucket has five of them," Alicia explained, "and together they function as a sort of mayor. You have to get elected."

At the museum entrance Alicia took out a key ring from her pocket. She unlocked the door, then stepped inside to punch in the alarm code on a panel. "That's weird," she said, frowning. "Someone must have forgotten to put on the alarm."

Frank, Joe, and Callie followed Alicia inside. Suddenly Joe heard footsteps on the mezzanine. "There's someone else here!" he said. "Come on, Frank—let's check it out."

Joe rushed forward into the dark room, with

Frank right behind. As Joe reached the bottom of the stairway, he could see something on the balcony. Silhouetted in the moonlight, it looked like a monster with all its arms waving.

The next thing Joe knew, a huge black object was falling down on him!

3 A Shocking Announcement

Frank tackled Joe and pushed him forward. The huge black object landed behind them with a thud. It was the octopus, they realized.

"Ugh," Joe said, looking as though he wanted to gag, "this thing stinks. And it's got its arms all over me." He removed two tentacles, which had fallen over his legs. "I guess taxidermy doesn't make it a cuddly kid's toy."

"Come on," Frank said, jumping to his feet. "Whoever's in here threw that on you. We've got to find out who it is." Frank's sneakers scudded on the floor as he took off up the stairs.

"Callie, Alicia!" Joe called as softly as he could. "We're going to look around. Can you turn on some lights?" Alicia flicked on the light switch by the main entrance as Joe dashed up the stairs behind Frank.

"I can't believe it!" Frank exclaimed when he reached the top. Before him lay the ruins of the shipwreck exhibit. Display cabinets had been smashed, and shards of glass were everywhere. Ship models had been knocked off their display tables and lay in broken pieces among the glass.

"I wonder if anything's been stolen," Frank said. "Alicia might know—"

A crash interrupted him. It came from Mr. Geovanis's office, and it sounded to Frank like glass breaking.

Frank and Joe took off down the mezzanine toward the closed office door. Joe was about to fling the door open when Frank grabbed his arm. "Whoever's inside might have a weapon," he cautioned.

Positioning themselves on either side of the door, the Hardys listened for a moment. Everything was silent. Frank pushed the door open a crack and peered inside. He could see that the computer monitor was on, giving off an eerie glow in the darkness.

Frank opened the door farther, while Joe switched on the overhead light. The room looked empty.

"What happened here?" Joe said with a low whistle. The office was a wreck. Manuscripts and books were scattered everywhere. File drawers had been opened, and papers were strewn on the floor. Glass from a broken picture frame lay in tiny pieces on the desk.

"Make sure no one's hiding behind the desk," Frank said as he and Joe strode into the room.

"No sign of anyone," Joe said, leaning over the desk.

A breeze wafted through the room. "Joe, look," Frank said, pointing to the far corner.

A window, partially hidden by a bookshelf, was wide open. "He must have escaped that way." Frank moved over to the window and leaned out. A fire escape led down the side of the old brick building to a deserted alley.

"Not a soul in sight," he said. "The guy must be long gone." Frank brought his head back inside.

"Take a look at this," Joe said as he stood in front of the computer.

"It looks like the main menu of files," Frank said, coming up next to Joe. The cursor highlighted a file labeled Fundra.97. Frank clicked the mouse, and a list of fund-raising events for the current year flashed onto the screen. "Can you make anything of this, Joe?"

Joe's blue eyes looked puzzled. "Nope," he said. "At least, not yet. Give me a few more minutes."

"You stay here, then," Frank said. "I'm going to tell Callie and Alicia it's okay to come up."

Joe gave Frank the thumbs-up sign, his eyes on the computer screen.

Two minutes later Frank, Callie, and Alicia came in. Alicia's face was sheet white, and her green eyes flashed with anger. "Can you tell whether anything's missing?" Frank asked her.

Alicia shook her head. "I can't tell anything right now. I hate to think how Dad's going to take this." She sat down in her father's desk chair.

"I can't make sense of these files to see if the intruder was looking for a specific thing," Joe said. "And I haven't noticed anything that might clue us in to his or her identity."

"Identity!" Alicia scoffed. "Isn't it clear that the culprit is Roberto Scarlatti?"

"No," Frank said firmly. "We have no hard evidence pointing to Scarlatti. We don't even have evidence that the person took anything."

"Hang on a second," Joe said. He ducked into the hallway and walked down the corridor to the next office. "Bingo," he breathed as he read the placard next to the door: Roberto Scarlatti, Assistant Curator.

Joe opened the door and flicked on the light switch, then stepped inside. "Wow," he said to himself. "This guy makes the army look disorganized."

Scarlatti's office was a model of order. The only items on his desk were a blotter, an inkstand, and a conch shell serving as a paperweight for a pile of neatly stacked notepaper. Not even a spot of ink on the blotter, Joe thought as he shook his head in disbelief.

When he stepped back into the corridor, Joe saw Frank, Callie, and Alicia looking at the broken display cases in the exhibit area.

"Scarlatti wins the neatness award of the year," Joe said as he joined them. "And his office hasn't been touched."

"That's even more proof that Scarlatti's behind all this," Alicia said hotly. "He wouldn't have wrecked his own stuff."

"But why would Scarlatti trash the museum?" Frank asked. "He may be angry at your father and want his job, but how would this get Scarlatti what he wants?"

Alicia shrugged, peering into one of the display cases. "Roberto really went off the deep end yesterday—it would figure that he'd go to more extremes today." She paused, then went on. "I'm almost positive that some cutlery and plates are missing from the *Titanic* exhibit. They're not in here, and I haven't noticed them anywhere on the floor." She moved off in the direction of her father's office.

"Hmm," Callie said. "Then it looks like the person's motive may have been theft. Maybe he or she was on the way to Scarlatti's office but heard us coming."

"Or it could have been Scarlatti on some crazy mission of revenge, trying to cover his tracks by making it seem like a robbery," Joe suggested.

"I want to look around some more for clues before we call the police," Frank said.

"Then you're going to have to hurry," Alicia said, sticking her head out of her father's office. "I just called the police and they're coming immediately. I also put in a call to Jonah Ferrier's house. He's the editor-in-chief of the *Island News*, and he's hosting the dinner that Dad went to tonight. I left a message for Dad to come to the museum pronto."

"Then let's get going, guys," Frank urged. Leaning over the balcony by the stairs, Frank saw that the stuffed octopus had been attached to the ceiling by a chain with a hook on the end. The hook, now empty, dangled over the cavernous museum space at about the level of Frank's waist. All the intruder had to do was reach over the balcony and unhook the thing, Frank figured.

"Nantucket police!" announced a voice from downstairs. Two police officers—a thin middle-aged man and a chubby younger one—entered the museum lobby and began to climb the stairs toward Frank. "I'm Detective Crespi," the older man said, "and this is my partner, Officer Brunswick. I understand you've had a bit of trouble here."

After introducing himself, Frank told the police what had happened. Then he introduced them to Joe, Callie, and Alicia.

"Thank you for coming so quickly," Alicia told the officers as she led the way to her father's office.

"Just doing our job," Detective Crespi said brusquely. "Now, while Officer Brunswick takes a look around, let me ask you all a few questions. First, were there any signs of forced entry?"

Alicia told them that the door was locked when they arrived but the alarm had been off.

"So it was probably someone who's familiar with the alarm code," Crespi guessed. "Do all the employees know it?"

"The higher-level ones do—like my dad and Mr. Scarlatti, the assistant curator," Alicia answered. "I do part-time work here, so I have a key and know the code."

When Detective Crespi asked Alicia if she knew whether anything had been stolen, she mentioned the cutlery and china from the *Titanic*. "But I can't tell whether anything's missing from Dad's office," she added.

Holding a pad of yellow paper with notes scrawled on it, Officer Brunswick joined the group. "There's nothing more we can do until we talk to your father," he said, looking at Alicia. "Please have him contact us as soon as possible.

He'll be the one to know for sure if anything's been stolen."

"How about dusting for fingerprints?" Joe suggested. "The broken window frame might be a good place because none of us touched it."

"Good idea," Crespi said. "I'll do that now—and then I think we can call it a night. Of course, we'll have to close the museum until it's cleaned up and an inventory is taken."

After the police had finished their work, Alicia locked up the museum. Then she hopped on her bicycle and headed toward home, while Frank and Joe walked Callie to her apartment door.

The Hardys strolled back to the Great White Whale, their bed-and-breakfast, carrying their skateboards and thinking about the case so far. When they reached the inn, they nearly fell into their beds, exhausted from the events of their day on the usually calm island of Nantucket.

"Now, this is what I call a breakfast," Joe said as he attacked a pile of pancakes the next morning. He and Frank were sitting at a table in the breakfast room of the Great White Whale.

"You'd better not go swimming today, Joe," Frank said slyly, "or you'll sink like—"

Frank stopped in midsentence as the front door to the inn crashed open and Alicia appeared in the doorway of the breakfast room.

"Alicia!" Joe said. "What's up?"

Alicia's face looked frozen with fear. She rushed into the room. "Frank, Joe," she said in a shaky voice. "I need your help. Dad's disappeared. He never came home from last night's dinner!"

4 Deadbeat Dune Buggy

"What?" Joe exclaimed. He stood up and put an arm around Alicia, then settled her into a chair next to him and Frank. Alicia took several deep breaths, then buried her face in her hands.

"Alicia," Frank said gravely, "tell us what happened after we all left the museum last night."

Lifting her head, Alicia stared into space for a few moments. Frank could tell she was struggling to stay calm. "Let's see," she began in a shaky voice. "As you know, Dad never showed up at the museum, so I decided to wait for him at home. Well"—she paused, her lip trembling—"he never came home."

33

"Did you check in again with the people who gave the dinner party?" Joe asked.

"Yes," Alicia said. "I called the Ferriers right away when I got home, and this time Mr. Ferrier told me that he hadn't seen Dad since dinner. When I had called earlier from the museum, some guest who didn't know anything took my message. She hadn't realized that Dad had already left."

"Have you told the police?" Frank asked her.

"Yes," Alicia said. "I called them right away, after I spoke to Mr. Ferrier. Dad could have still been out somewhere, but I was worried. I know it was way too early to file a missing-persons report or anything, but I thought the police would do something because of the museum break-in."

"It's true," Joe observed. "Your dad's disappearance and the wrecked museum seem as though they've got to be linked. Anyway, let's just say the two events happening on the same night make for a weird coincidence."

Alicia nodded in agreement. "That's what I thought, too. When I called the police, they said I could file a missing-persons report, but I'd have to wait twenty-four hours for him to be officially considered missing."

"Did you talk to Detective Crespi?" Frank asked.

"Yes," Alicia said. "He was sympathetic and everything, but he said that my dad might have

34

just been out with friends and that I shouldn't worry. He told me to make sure that my dad called him the minute he got home. He seemed more concerned that Dad wasn't around to answer questions about the museum vandalism."

"And Crespi didn't speculate that the two events might be linked?" Frank pressed.

Alicia shook her head. "No. The vandalism was on his mind, not my dad."

"Well, his tune might change in another twenty-four hours," Joe said grimly. "Though I hope Crespi is right—that your dad was just out with friends."

Alicia drew a deep breath, then let it out in a slow sigh. "That's not Dad's style—to party all night," she said. "And even if he had been with friends, he'd call me to let me know he'd be home late."

Frank knew Alicia was right. He could understand Geovanis staying out late with friends, but it was odd that he hadn't called by now. Something may have happened to him—either an accident, or a crime.

"Anyway," Alicia went on, "I barely slept all night, and by nine this morning when Dad still wasn't home, I knew something was really wrong. I'm convinced he's been kidnapped—and that Roberto Scarlatti's the culprit!"

"Alicia," Frank said, "you can't jump to conclusions like that. I agree your dad could be in some sort of trouble. But he may have been in a car accident or something. Have you checked the hospital?"

"Of course," Alicia replied, looking exasperated. "And he's not there. Besides, the police would have told me that. Also, Jonah Ferrier told me that my red Jeep, which Dad had borrowed last night because his car was being fixed, is still sitting outside the Ferrier house."

Frank and Joe were silent for a moment while they thought about Alicia's story. Finally Joe said, "Let's say your dad was kidnapped. Maybe the guy kidnapped him first, then went into the museum to trash it. But why?"

"*If* it was the same person," Frank pointed out. "We're just guessing here—we have no evidence yet—"

"But I'd say my guess is a pretty educated one," Joe cut in. "What are the odds that Geovanis would get kidnapped and the museum vandalized all in one night, by two different guys with different motives?"

Frank shrugged. "I see what you mean."

"It must be Roberto Scarlatti, then," Alicia pressed. "He's the only enemy my father has. Everyone else loves him."

Frank rubbed his chin thoughtfully. It may seem like Geovanis is a popular guy, he thought, but that doesn't mean he has no other enemies.

"You guys will help me investigate, right?"

Alicia pleaded. "You're my only hope at this point."

"Of course we will," Frank said, smiling. "And we should get going right away—to chase down Scarlatti and also talk to Jonah Ferrier."

"So you agree with me about Scarlatti?" Alicia asked hopefully.

"Kind of," Frank answered. "I agree that Scarlatti is jealous of your dad, and his behavior yesterday in the museum points to him as the likely culprit. Also, the trashing of your dad's office and not Scarlatti's makes the guy look guilty. But why would Scarlatti want to wreck the museum he wants to take over?"

Joe pushed back his chair and got to his feet. "I'm tired of these guessing games. Let's go check out Scarlatti's house. Since the museum's closed, he might be at home."

"Do you know where he lives?" Frank asked Alicia as they both stood up.

"He lives in Siasconset—or 'Sconset as the people who live here call it," Alicia told him. "I'll lead you there on my moped."

"Great," Joe said. "Frank and I can borrow mopeds from the inn."

Five minutes later Frank, Joe, and Alicia were speeding to 'Sconset on mopeds. Since the main road was being resurfaced just outside the village, they were forced to detour onto a rutted road.

The road was narrow and treacherous, with sharp curves and cliffs that plummeted down to a rocky shoreline twenty feet below. Glancing out over the ocean, Frank could see the colorful jibs of sailboats zigzagging across the choppy blue water. The faint hum of a plane in the distance grew steadily louder.

Suddenly the noise became overwhelming. It wasn't a plane, Frank realized—it was some vehicle behind him revving its motor.

"Watch where you're going!" Frank heard Joe shout.

Frank shot a quick glance behind him. A blue dune buggy with a red lobster insignia on the hood was bearing down on Joe, as if trying to push him off the winding road. Frank knew he had to act fast, or Joe would plummet down the cliff.

Frank slammed on his brakes, hoping it would force the fast-moving dune buggy to swerve and pass them both.

Frank looked quickly over his shoulder and then back at the road ahead of him. His heart leaped into his throat. The road had curved and he'd veered into the other lane—right into the path of an oncoming car!

5 Hang-Up Call

At the last possible second Frank steered his moped hard to the right and missed the oncoming car by inches. Back in the right lane, he brought the moped to a halt on the side of the road.

"Hey, buddy, you okay?" the driver yelled as he slowed his car. "You'd better be careful or you'll drive right into the water."

"Sorry," Frank said. He shot a glance over his left shoulder to see the blue blur of the dune buggy speeding by him.

"Frank!" Joe yelled from behind. Frank turned to see that Joe had stopped his moped about ten yards behind. His blue eyes were flashing with anger, and his breath came in bursts.

"Did you see that yahoo?" Joe asked "He was trying to run me off the road—he looked like he was planning to pick you off next."

"I saw the dune buggy but not the driver," Frank told him. "Did you get a look at him?"

"Nope," Joe said, shaking his head. "I was too busy trying to stay on the road."

"Hey, guys, what's going on?" Alicia shouted as she approached them from the opposite direction. "I noticed you weren't behind me, so I turned back." She wheeled her moped around, bringing it to a stop next to Joe's.

"Did you see a bright blue dune buggy go by you on the road?" Frank asked her. "It nearly knocked Joe over the cliff—and almost made me slam into a car."

"Did it have a picture of a lobster on the front of the hood?" Alicia asked.

"That's the one," Frank told her. "Did you see the driver?"

"Not very well—he was really speeding. But it looked like he was wearing some kind of hat or mask or something," she said, furrowing her brow. "It was pretty weird."

"That's for sure." Joe looked troubled. "That driver definitely had it in for us—and he didn't want to be recognized." Joe blew out his breath. "It looks like somebody's trying to warn us off the case."

"But who could know about our investigation at this stage?" Frank mused. "We were the only ones in the breakfast room at the Great White Whale."

"It's true—you guys have been on the case for less than an hour," Alicia said. "No one else could possibly know about it."

Frank looked thoughtful. "Except for one person. Whoever dropped the octopus on me and Joe last night probably got a look at us—from the moonlight coming through the windows. The guy may easily guess that we're helping you out, Alicia."

"We're near 'Sconset. Roberto could be on the lookout for us—while he's trying to guard Dad," Alicia said.

"Scarlatti—or whoever kidnapped your father—might have learned from your dad that we're detectives," Frank said. "He might have wormed that information out of him."

Alicia glanced anxiously from Frank to Joe. "What do you mean—'wormed' it out of him? I hope he's being treated nicely and not forced to give out information—"

"Alicia," Joe cut in. "We need your help to find your dad, so you've got to try to stay calm." He frowned at Frank, wishing his brother hadn't brought up the subject of how Mr. Geovanis was being treated.

"I'm sure your dad's fine," Frank said, understanding Joe's warning frown. "Kidnappers usually want something from other people—money or whatever—so it's in their best interest to treat their captives well. Then they can exchange their captive for whatever it is they want."

"I'm sorry to get upset," Alicia said with a quick smile. "It's just that I'm so worried."

"It's totally understandable," Joe said. He gripped the handlebars of his moped and began to move slowly forward.

"We'd better get a move on," Frank said, as he revved up his bike. "Every minute counts."

Ten minutes later Frank, Joe, and Alicia parked their mopeds on a narrow street in the tiny fishing village of 'Sconset. As Alicia scouted around for the house, Frank and Joe studied their surroundings. The village was set on a bluff overlooking the Atlantic Ocean, and the Hardys noticed that 'Sconset was much smaller and less crowded than the town of Nantucket.

After walking by a row of modest cottages surrounded by picket fences thick with roses, they stopped in front of a much larger house surrounded by a wide green lawn. The house was white with black shutters and a wraparound porch. Two dramatic-looking turrets stuck out on either side of its third story.

"This is it," Alicia announced. "Scarlatti's house."

"Nice place!" Joe exclaimed.

"It's a reproduction of a ship captain's house," Alicia told Frank and Joe. "There are a bunch of houses like this in the town of Nantucket, dating from the late 1700s when Nantucket was one of the major whaling ports of the world. Roberto admired them, but he wanted to live in 'Sconset for the view so he had one built."

"What are those towers for?" Frank asked.

"I think they were for spotting ships at sea, or maybe even whales," Alicia answered.

Joe grinned, then rushed up the porch stairs. "Come on, guys. Let's see if we can spot anything in this house."

Frank rang the doorbell, then gave the door a hard knock. When no one answered, he tried the door handle. The door was locked.

Joe walked to the end of the porch on the right side of the house and craned his head over the lawn, scouting around for the dune buggy.

"If it was Scarlatti in that dune buggy," Joe said as he walked back to Frank and Alicia, "he must still be out in it. I don't see a garage back here, and the dune buggy's definitely not on the street."

"He could be hiding it somewhere," Frank

43

suggested. "But you're right—the guy doesn't seem to be at home." Turning to Alicia, Frank asked, "Do you know what kind of car Scarlatti usually drives?"

"I'm not positive, but I think it's some kind of plain gray car," Alicia said. "I remember him giving Dad a ride home in it once."

"There's no gray car parked on the street," Frank said, glancing from one side of the street to the other.

"Should we try to sneak in and look around?" Joe asked. "There may be a window open somewhere."

"There also may be a secret passageway," Alicia said. "Roberto's always bragged about what an exact reproduction his house is, and that it even has a secret passageway."

"A secret passageway?" Joe asked. "Cool."

"Yes. I've heard that some old Nantucket houses have them," Alicia said. "I don't know whether Roberto's really exists or where it leads, but should we take a look around for it?"

"Later," Frank said, looking at his watch. "First we should check out your house, Alicia. Maybe the kidnapper's left some kind of message there."

"Let's go," Joe said, taking the porch stairs two at a time.

"Wait a minute," Alicia said as she and Frank

caught up to Joe on the sidewalk. "Could we pick up my Jeep at the Ferriers' house first? My cell phone's in the glove compartment, and I wouldn't want to leave it on the street for too long. Also, there might be a clue in the Jeep about Dad."

"Good idea," Frank said. "But wouldn't your father have the keys?"

"I've got an extra set," Alicia said, patting her shorts pocket.

Half an hour later Alicia, Frank, and Joe dropped off their mopeds at the Great White Whale, then walked three blocks down Fair Street to where Alicia's Jeep was parked.

"That's Jonah Ferrier's house," Alicia said, pointing to a white clapboard house with green shutters. "Do you think we should talk to him about when he last saw Dad?"

Frank heard a ringing sound. "My phone!" Alicia said. Fumbling with her keys, Alicia rushed to unlock the glove compartment. Then she grabbed the phone. "Hello?" she said into the receiver. "Dad! Dad, is that you?"

As Frank and Joe waited tensely, Alicia shouted, "Dad, where are you?"

She paused for a moment, covering her right ear with her hand as she struggled to hear. "Talk louder," she pleaded.

Alicia straightened up, then shook the phone

in desperation. She put it back against her ear. "Hello? Hello?"

She looked at Frank and Joe, her eyes wide with terror. "It was Dad. He's been kidnapped—I know it."

6 Who's the Hot Rod?

Frank gently took the phone from Alicia and put it to his ear. The line was dead. Discouraged, he handed it back to Alicia, who put it in her backpack. "I'm keeping this with me at all times, in case Dad calls again," she said.

"I wonder if your dad could have seen us and that's why he called at that moment," Frank said. He peered at Jonah Ferrier's house, wondering if Mr. Geovanis could have called from somewhere inside. A breeze from an open window ruffled a curtain in one of the top floor windows, but Frank saw no signs of life.

"Maybe it was just a coincidence," Joe said.

"Could be," Frank said. Turning to Alicia, he

said, "Tell us exactly what you heard. First, are you sure it was your dad?"

"Positive," Alicia said. "These were his exact words: 'Alicia, it's Dad. I need help.' Then he said something I couldn't hear, and the line went dead."

"Did you hear anything else in the background—anything that could give us a clue to his whereabouts?" Joe asked.

Alicia shook her head. "He was there one moment and gone the next. That's it." Alicia pressed her lips into a thin line. "I can't believe this is happening," she whispered.

"Take it easy," Joe said. "We'll find your father. I know it."

"You really think so?" Alicia asked, glancing at Joe.

"Of course we will," Joe said, trying to sound as confident as he could. "Look, Alicia," he went on, "Nantucket's an island. It's not that easy getting off it, especially in the summer with all the crowds. Frank and I couldn't even get a ferry reservation to bring our van over."

"You're right," Alicia said. "It would be hard for anyone to get last-minute plane reservations, or car reservations on the ferry. But what if the kidnapper takes Dad on the ferry and has a car waiting on the mainland—on Cape Cod?"

Joe furrowed his brow. "How could a kidnapper force your father onto a ferry full of people? That would be a little obvious."

"True," Alicia said. "So odds are Dad's still on the island."

"You bet," Joe said, nodding.

Alicia lifted her chin, her eyes filled with determination. "I'll find Dad wherever he is— whatever it takes. I won't rest until I do."

While they were talking, Frank strode up the path to Jonah's house. "Where are you going?" Joe asked him.

"Just thought I'd take a look around," Frank answered, knocking on the front door. "After all, Mr. Geovanis was last seen here. And his phone call came the instant we arrived at the house. He could have been watching for us."

When no one answered his knock, Frank peered through the open window to the right of the door. Inside was a living room with a door opening onto a garden in back. A gate in a hedge led to another street.

"Whoever kidnapped Alicia's father might have lured him into the garden and then taken him through that back gate to a waiting car," Joe said, looking over Frank's shoulder.

"Could be," Frank said, nodding. "But just to be sure, why don't we take a look inside—see if Mr. Geovanis is there?"

At that moment a curly-haired boy about

49

twelve or thirteen strolled up the path. "Can I help you?" he asked.

"We're looking for Jonah Ferrier," Frank said, smiling at the boy. "I'm Frank Hardy, this is my brother, Joe, and this is Alicia Geovanis."

"I'm Jamie Ferrier," the boy said. "Mr. Ferrier's my dad." He searched in his pocket for a moment, then fished out a key. "He's usually at the newspaper Saturday afternoons getting ready for the Sunday edition. You could probably find him there."

"Were you at your parents' party last night, by any chance?" Joe asked him.

"Nope. I slept over at a friend's house." Jamie started to unlock the door. "Nice to meet you, but I have to go."

Back inside the Jeep Frank, Joe, and Alicia talked about what to do next. Alicia wanted to go straight home to see if the kidnapper—or her father—had left any messages. Frank wanted to stop off first at the *Island News* to ask Jonah Ferrier some questions. The newspaper office was on the way to Alicia's house, he pointed out. Callie was there, and Frank wanted to see if she could join them for the afternoon.

"Why don't you call your answering machine at home, Alicia?" Joe suggested. "You could do that from your car phone, right?"

"Good idea," Alicia said. She took out the

phone and punched in some numbers. After a moment she clicked it shut. "No messages. So let's stop off first at the *Island News.*"

Joe swiveled around to face the backseat. "Are you considering Jonah Ferrier a suspect?" he asked Frank.

"No, not really," Frank replied. "But Mr. Geovanis *was* last seen at Ferrier's house and he *did* call on Alicia's phone when we were outside. He no doubt knows she usually keeps her phone in her Jeep."

"I can't imagine what motive Jonah Ferrier would have for hiding Dad in his house," Alicia said as she started up the Jeep. "Roberto's the one with the ax to grind."

"You're right," Frank said. "But we still need to find out what Ferrier knows about last night. He might remember an important clue."

After a few minutes Alicia pulled her Jeep up in front of the offices of the *Island News* near the corner of Main and Easy Streets. She switched off the ignition, then immediately waved to a ruddy-faced man with curly dark hair who was on his way out of the newspaper building.

"Hey there, honey," the man said in a loud voice. He flashed Alicia a grin, his mischievous-looking blue eyes twinkling at her. "Haven't seen you in a dog's age."

"Hi, Jonah," Alicia said. She hopped out of the

Jeep and shook his hand. "These are my friends, Frank and Joe Hardy. This is Jonah Ferrier, editor-in-chief of the *Island News*."

Frank and Joe climbed out of the Jeep and shook hands with Jonah Ferrier. Joe judged he was in his midthirties.

"Nice to meet you," Jonah said as he pumped Joe's hand.

Ow! Joe thought. That guy has some handshake. Joe gave Ferrier a friendly smile but at the same time studied him carefully. There was something about Ferrier's too-friendly manner that Joe didn't trust.

Taking note of Ferrier's brightly colored clothes—green pants embroidered with tiny whales and a pink Lacoste shirt—Joe thought the guy sure knew how to draw attention.

"I saw your old man last night," Jonah told Alicia.

"I know that," Alicia said. "And I talked to you this morning on the phone, remember? I asked you when you'd last seen Dad, because he never came home from your party."

"Oh, yes," Jonah said, thumping his forehead with his fist. "Of course, you did call. Sorry I didn't remember, but I've had a lot on my mind lately. Did your father ever come home?"

"Not yet," Alicia told him. "We're all pretty anxious about it."

"Don't worry, darlin'," Jonah said, patting her mop of red curls. "I'm sure your father will show up soon. He was probably out having a good time. After all, the man deserves to kick up his heels every once in a while."

Joe gritted his teeth as he listened to Ferrier's casual tone. It was all he could do not to slug the guy. Couldn't he tell Alicia was worried sick?

Looking over at Frank, Joe was trying to gauge his brother's reaction to Ferrier's manner. Frank was staring poker-faced at Ferrier, but Joe knew Frank was probably just as turned off by the guy's attitude as he was.

"So you held the party last night where Mr. Geovanis was last seen," Frank commented. "Do you know what time he left?"

"Hmm," Ferrier said, scrunching up his face as he thought. "I remember George filling his plate with food from the buffet around eight o'clock. That was in the dining room. About ten minutes later I heard George arguing in the hallway with another man. It sounded like Harrison Cartwright, the man I hosted the party for."

"Did you hear what they were saying?" Joe asked, curious.

Ferrier shook his head. "I wish I could help you, son."

Joe stifled another urge to bury his fist in Ferrier's face. He couldn't quite put his finger on why the guy bugged him so much—maybe because he seemed so phony, Joe thought.

"Did you see Mr. Geovanis after that?" Frank asked.

Ferrier sighed. "I had so much to think about last night—I was running around like a chicken with its head cut off. The truth is, I don't remember seeing George after that incident, but I do remember seeing Harrison. He made a speech shortly after dessert."

"And what time was that?" Frank pressed.

"You guys!" Ferrier said, rolling his eyes in exasperation. "What is this—twenty questions?"

"Jonah," Alicia said, her voice icier than Joe had ever heard it. "We're just trying to figure out where Dad went. Don't you want to help us?"

Ferrier gave Alicia a look of surprise, then fixed her with a condescending stare. "You're getting to be quite a tough young lady." He sighed, then added, "Dessert was served at around nine, but I really don't remember much else. As I said, I was extremely busy."

"Did Mr. Geovanis talk to anyone else in particular?" Frank asked. "Or don't you remember?"

"George talked to everyone," Jonah answered. "He's a sociable guy, and many of his friends were there. But other than his talk with Harrison in the hallway, I don't think he had any special conversation with anyone."

"Thanks, Mr. Ferrier," Frank said. "Please let us know if you remember anything else."

"I certainly will." Ferrier started to walk away. Then he turned around, his eyes gleaming with sudden interest. "You've asked me some questions," he began, "and now it's my turn to ask you a few. Did you hear what happened to the shipping museum last night?"

"You mean the break-in?" Alicia asked.

"You bet. I have a reporter there covering it as we speak. Who would do such a dreadful thing?" Ferrier's glance darted from Alicia to Joe to Frank.

"I also heard the balloon may be a hoax," Ferrier went on. "The paper ran an article today quoting Roberto Scarlatti on the subject. I wonder how your father's going to take all this?" His blue eyes studied Alicia curiously—a bit too curiously, Joe thought—as if the guy wanted the article to upset Alicia, too.

Before Alicia had time to answer him, Callie showed up. "Hi, guys. Hello, Mr. Ferrier," she said. To her friends, she added, "I'm doing a story about the Corn Mill for tomorrow's paper. Do you want to come with me?"

"See you all around," Ferrier said, clapping Joe on the back. "I'm late for lunch." He ambled across the street to a row of parked cars.

Joe followed him with his eyes. "No!" Joe said suddenly. "I can't believe it."

Across the street Jonah Ferrier was climbing into a blue dune buggy with a red lobster insignia on the front—identical to the one that had run them off the road earlier!

7 Set for Sabotage

Joe grabbed Frank's arm. "Jonah Ferrier was the nut who tried to push us off the road!" he said.

"It appears that way," Frank said grimly as he watched Ferrier drive down Easy Street.

"What are you guys talking about?" Callie asked.

"We'll fill you in later," Joe said. "We've got to follow that dune buggy. Alicia, will you let me drive? I think I saw where he went."

Alicia tossed Joe her keys, then she scrambled into the backseat of the Jeep beside Callie. "Hurry or we'll lose him!" Frank said, strapping himself into the seat next to Joe. Joe pulled out of the parking space and headed down Easy Street.

"He's up there," Frank said, "about to head up Oak Street."

Joe caught a glimpse of a bright blue vehicle wheeling to the left a couple blocks ahead. "Hang on!" he shouted as he pressed the accelerator. The Jeep lurched forward.

A crowd of tourists was crossing the street at the crosswalk in front of him. Joe gritted his teeth in frustration.

"Chill out, Joe," Frank said. "You don't want to mow people down just to get Ferrier."

"I know, I know," Joe said. "I just don't want to lose that bozo."

Finally all the pedestrians made it across the street, and Joe was able to move forward again. But by the time he reached Oak Street, there was no sign of Ferrier anywhere. Cruising up the street, Joe craned his head from side to side. It was as though Ferrier had disappeared into thin air. Joe brought the Jeep to a stop in a parking space. "Now what?" he asked.

"You could start by letting me know what this is all about," Callie said.

Frank quickly told Callie about the events of the morning, starting with George Geovanis's disappearance. After he finished, Callie stared at Alicia in amazement. "Your father's been kidnapped?"

Alicia nodded gravely. "We haven't heard from the kidnapper yet, but we're assuming that's what happened. There's no other explanation for Dad to be gone so long."

Callie frowned. "He could have been in an accident, Alicia."

"But what about the dune buggy driver, and Dad's phone call to me?" Alicia pointed out. "Someone wants Frank and Joe off the trail."

"But I can't believe the driver of that dune buggy was Mr. Ferrier," Callie protested. "He may be loud and obnoxious sometimes, but he wouldn't kidnap anyone, or run anyone off the road."

Joe laughed in disbelief. "A regular guy, huh? All of us saw Ferrier get into the same car that tried to run us off the road. There couldn't be more of those lobster paint jobs on the island."

Callie shrugged. "There could be." She paused, then added, "But what's Mr. Ferrier's motive?"

"Has your dad ever argued with Jonah Ferrier?" Frank asked Alicia. "Do they get along?"

Alicia looked thoughtful. "They barely know each other, but they seem to get along. Jonah's the type who's friendly to everyone."

"Can you think of any reason why he'd want to trash the museum?" Frank asked.

"No," Alicia replied. "But Jonah does have a reputation for being a prankster. He's been known to pull pranks to get publicity around newspaper subscription time." She frowned for a moment. "I know this sounds far-fetched, but could he be hiding my father just to get a hot story?"

Joe's jaw dropped. "You think he's that desperate for a story? What kind of pranks has he pulled?"

"Last year he let loose a herd of pigs at a meeting in the town hall," Alicia said. "He got some good stories out of that one, and apparently subscriptions went up."

"Maybe he also cooked up the balloon hoax," Joe mused, "if it is a hoax."

"I don't know, guys," Frank said, shaking his head. "It does sound far-fetched to think that he's doing all this just to beef up newspaper subscriptions. Kidnapping isn't a prank, either. It's a really serious crime."

"Mr. Ferrier would have to keep his identity secret from Mr. Geovanis," Callie said, "or he'd be caught and sent to jail. Do you really think he'd go to all that trouble just for the newspaper?"

"Probably not," Frank said. "Still, I think the guy's definitely worth watching. Even if Ferrier doesn't have an obvious motive, Mr. Geovanis was last seen at his house, we got the phone call right there, and he does have that painted-up dune buggy. That's a lot of circumstantial evidence."

A bright blue vehicle stopped at the crossroads up ahead. It was the dune buggy with the red lobster insignia!

"Do you see what I see?" Joe asked.

"Yup," Frank said. "Go for it."

Joe started up the engine and accelerated out of the parking space. At that moment the dune buggy headed straight across the intersection on the street that crossed Oak Street. After stopping at the stop sign, Joe hung a left. The dune buggy was a block ahead.

"Do you think it's Ferrier?" Frank asked.

Joe hunched forward over the steering wheel, squinting against the sunlight reflected off the back of the buggy. "Look, Frank! The driver's wearing a cap—just like the guy who ran us off the road."

"Don't take your eyes off him," Frank said as the vehicle turned right up Main Street.

"Are you nuts? My eyeballs are glued to him." Joe pressed the accelerator, and the Jeep bumped along the cobblestone street, skirting bicyclists and pedestrians.

"He's heading left out of town," Callie said. "Hurry, or we'll lose him."

Joe wheeled the Jeep to the left onto a smoothly paved side street. The dune buggy was a shiny blue blur several blocks ahead.

"Gun it, Joe," Frank said. "He's getting away."

Joe switched to third gear as the traffic and pedestrians thinned out, and the Jeep roared up the empty road.

"Have we lost him?" Frank asked, leaning forward. He saw a flash of blue heading right as the road forked up ahead. "Joe, go right!"

"I can't—I'm going too fast!" Joe yelled as he sped down the left-hand fork.

"If you turn right at the next street, it will feed into the road you missed," Alicia said.

Joe slammed on the brakes as much as he dared. With a shower of sand and gravel, he turned the Jeep right.

The buggy was slowly bumping along ahead of them. "This road leads to the Corn Mill two miles down," Alicia explained.

"Don't get away from me now, buddy," Joe begged. He had stopped the Jeep for a moment, waiting for some bicyclists to move from the middle of the road. Just then the buggy disappeared around a curve. "Rats!" he exclaimed, punching the steering wheel. Finally the cyclists moved to the side, and Joe drove on.

"Do you see it anywhere?" Joe asked as he rounded a curve.

"Not yet," Alicia said. Three pairs of eyes scanned the empty road ahead as Joe gunned the accelerator.

"There!" Callie said. "To the right. It's parked

on that little road next to Mehanuck Pond—right by the Corn Mill."

Joe slowed. Sure enough, the buggy was parked in front of a small pond in the middle of a field.

"Bingo," Frank said. "We've got the car, but where's the driver?"

"Do you think he went into the Corn Mill?" Callie asked. Joe brought the Jeep to a halt behind the dune buggy, and he and Frank looked across the pond at the windmill, a gray-shingled building that looked to Frank like a pepper shaker. The sails spun around in the breeze.

Joe glanced at a row of bushes next to the parked cars. "He could be anywhere."

Frank's dark eyes flickered with sudden awareness. Turning to Callie, he said, "Ferrier knew we were headed to the Corn Mill. He was with us on the street when you invited us along."

"I still don't believe he's involved in this," she said. "I'm sure Scarlatti's the one."

"Whoever it is, I wonder what's up his sleeve," Joe said. "This whole setup strikes me as fishy."

"Maybe we shouldn't go in," Alicia said nervously. "I don't want to march into some trap this guy's rigged, like some sort of lamebrain."

Frank smiled. "Then why don't you stay in the Jeep?" he suggested. "That way we'll have all bases covered."

"Okay," Alicia said. She climbed back into the Jeep, then glanced around at the deserted field. "It's kind of creepy out here, too. There's no one else around."

"Give a shout if you need us," Joe said. "We'll be right inside."

Frank, Joe, and Callie strolled around the pond and up to the front door of the mill. Inside, the light was dim, and it took a moment for Frank's eyes to adjust. Narrow rays of sunlight slanted across the rustic wooden interior, highlighting a young man in a blue T-shirt and a Boston Red Sox cap worn backward. The front of his shirt was covered with yellow dust.

"Hi," he said cheerfully. "My name's Bob. I'm the guide here. Just let me know if you'd like a demonstration." He pointed to a sack filled with corn kernels.

Frank studied the grindstones. They were circular, about five feet in diameter, and the top stone was attached to a long wooden shaft powered by the sails at the top of the building. A chute led from the bottom stone to a hopper full of corn meal in the cellar below.

"I'd like a demonstration," Callie said. "And I'd also like to get an idea of the mill's history. I'm writing up a story for the paper."

"Okay," Bob said, scooping up some corn in a tin can. "Then let's begin our lesson."

"Are we the only ones in here?" Joe asked.

"Did anyone else come or go within the last ten minutes?"

"Not a soul," Bob said. "It's been a quiet day."

Frank glanced at Joe. "Let's check out the view upstairs," he suggested, glancing at a flight of stairs winding around the shaft. "You never know what we'll find."

Bob began pouring corn into a chute that funneled it onto the bottom stone. Using a lever, he lowered the top stone until it ground against the bottom stone. The corn made a crunching sound as the stones ground it.

While Callie listened to Bob, Frank led Joe up the steep, rickety stairway. As they approached the second floor, there was a sudden crack. The step was breaking.

"Joe!" Frank shouted as he fell. He grabbed desperately for something to hold. Fifteen feet below him, the heavy machinery was working away, ready to crush whatever—or whoever— came between the heavy grindstones.

8 Riptide

Frank grabbed the broken stair with his left hand. "Joe, help me," he called. "I'm going to fall."

As Frank dangled over the grindstones below, Joe grabbed Frank's left forearm, using all his strength to keep his brother from falling.

"I need help," Joe grunted, his face red. His muscular arms shook with the weight of Frank's body, and beads of sweat broke out on his forehead. Joe shouted for Bob, but the loud noise of the grindstones drowned out his voice.

With Joe holding his left arm, Frank was able to swing his right hand up through the opening and reach for the side of the stair. "I think I can make it," he gasped. "Pull as hard as you can."

Joe managed to haul Frank up another two inches. "I've got it," Frank said as he clutched Joe's arm with his right hand. With Joe's support, Frank was finally able to scramble up through the broken stair.

"That was close," Joe said, wiping his brow with the back of his hand.

"Too close," Frank said. "I thought I was going to become a corn muffin."

"I'm surprised Bob didn't notice. I guess the machinery's too loud. Come on," Joe said. "Let's check out the stair. Something tells me this isn't a case of dry rot."

The Hardys inspected the stair, running their fingers over the old wood. "Look at this, Frank," Joe said, examining the righthand side.

"Wow," Frank said as Joe pointed out rough jagged marks in the stair close to the wall. Tiny specks of sawdust lay close to the cracks in the wood. "It looks like someone took a saw to this stair but didn't want to be obvious about it."

"Yeah, someone like the dune buggy driver," Joe said. "He must have come in here."

Skipping the broken stair, Joe climbed to the second floor of the mill and looked out the window. "The buggy's gone. And Alicia's not in the Jeep," he called. "I hope nothing's happened to her."

Taking the stairs two at a time, Joe rushed down to the first floor. Frank, still feeling wobbly, followed at a slower pace, his eyes glancing over each nook and shadow of the mill interior. Nothing he saw seemed the least bit suspicious.

Downstairs, the Hardys found both Callie and Alicia listening to Bob.

"Whew," Joe said, as his eyes met Alicia's. "You're here. I didn't see you in your Jeep, and the dune buggy's gone. Frank and I got worried."

"I didn't like being out there alone, with that weird buggy parked in front of me," Alicia said. "So I decided to join Callie."

"Good move," Joe said. "And now that we know where you are, I'd like to know where that dune buggy is. Did you hear it drive away?"

"No," Alicia said, looking puzzled. "We didn't hear or see anything. I didn't even know it was gone until you told us."

Joe filled everyone in on what had happened to Frank upstairs. Callie and Alicia looked shocked, but Joe thought he detected a hint of guilt flicker through Bob's eyes. Looking straight at him, Joe asked, "Are you sure no one came in here during the ten minutes before we arrived?"

Bob's expression clouded over with worry. "Well," he mumbled, "to tell you the truth, I can't be absolutely sure. Right before you got here, I left for a couple of minutes to give directions to a cyclist on the main road. I suppose someone could have sneaked in then. No one was in here, and there's no rule that says I have to be at my post every second."

"Don't worry about it," Frank told him. "You were just trying to help. But there must have been some visitors to the mill earlier today. I can't believe we're the first ones."

Bob looked thoughtful. "As I said, it's been quiet for a Saturday. I guess everyone's at the beach. But there was a group of women about an hour ago."

"Did they go all the way upstairs?" Joe asked.

"Yes. They wandered around for a while, listened to my talk, and then went upstairs. But there were no accidents," Bob said.

Frank and Joe thanked Bob for his help. "You'd better get that stair fixed before anyone else goes up there," Frank added as he and the others headed for the door.

Back at the Jeep Alicia said, "You're right, Frank, to wonder about Jonah Ferrier. He was the only person who knew we were coming to the Corn Mill."

Frank nodded, but Callie shook her head. "I just don't buy it," she said. "Mr. Ferrier's a totally harmless guy. I know that from working with him." She stared at the others. "Am I the only one around here who's sticking up for him?"

"At this stage of the investigation," Joe said, "we each have to keep an open mind. And you've got to admit, Callie, that a lot of factors point to Ferrier as the culprit."

"One thing we can all agree on," Frank said. "Someone wants us off the case." He climbed into the backseat of the Jeep and sat next to Callie. "Why don't we find out where Ferrier went for lunch?" he suggested. "If he has an alibi, then we could rule him out."

"I want to get back home," Alicia said as she strapped herself into the driver's seat. "If either Dad or the kidnapper calls, I want to be there. If there's still no news, I'm notifying the police." She thought for a moment. "Let's stop at the inn and I'll pick up my moped. Then you guys can borrow my Jeep to check out Jonah and join me at home later."

"Good thinking," Joe said. "Let's get moving."

Back at the *Island News* Callie introduced Frank and Joe to Jonah Ferrier's secretary, a gray-haired woman with a loud, confident manner. "I'm absolutely certain Jonah had lunch at the Jared Coffin House this afternoon," she told them. "It's the hotel a few blocks away. Jonah eats in the taproom there every Saturday with Katie Hall, the publisher of the *Island News.* You can always call the maître d' if you don't believe me."

"Why would he have driven there if it's only a few blocks from here?" Frank asked her.

The secretary frowned. "He sometimes delivers copy to Katie, who doesn't always come in on Saturday. And he gives her stacks of books and magazines to read for the weekend."

"Do you know where Mr. Ferrier bought his dune buggy?" Joe asked. "It's got an unusual design on the hood."

"Yes, it certainly does," she agreed. "I've seen one or two others on the island, but not many. There's a dealer named Freddie Applegate who lives near the airport. He paints Nantucket themes, like whales and lobsters, on motorcycles and dune buggies. That's where Jonah bought his."

Callie and the Hardys thanked her, then headed downstairs to use Callie's phone. Once he got there, Frank punched in the number of the Jared Coffin House. After a few questions to the maître d', Frank hung up. "Ferrier's there, all right," he told them with a shrug. "He's been chowing down for the past two hours."

"See?" Callie said triumphantly. "There's no way Mr. Ferrier could have sabotaged the stair. I knew he was in the clear."

"Unless he had an accomplice who borrowed the buggy for a few minutes just to lure us to the mill," Frank pointed out.

Callie rolled her eyes. "Frank Hardy, will you never give up?"

"Nope," Frank said, grinning. "Not until we

know for sure what's going on. Come on, let's head over to Alicia's."

"I'd also like to track down Harrison Cartwright," Joe said. "We should find out what he and Mr. Geovanis were arguing about last night."

"You guys go on," Callie said. "I've got to stay here and finish my work for the afternoon."

After Frank and Joe said goodbye to Callie, they hopped into Alicia's Jeep and headed off toward her house.

On the way through town, Joe took a quick detour and steered the Jeep by the Jared Coffin House. Ferrier's dune buggy was parked outside, with a stack of magazines in the backseat.

"Hmm," Joe said. "Ferrier's off the hook for the moment, I guess."

"Unless you go for my accomplice idea," Frank reminded him.

As Frank and Joe talked, Frank realized that their list of clues and suspects was growing shorter. Roberto Scarlatti was still the most likely suspect, but why would he wreck his own museum? *This case needs a break* bad, Frank thought.

Ten minutes out of town the houses thinned out and grassy dunes spilled down to the ocean. Joe pulled the Jeep into a sandy driveway at the end of a long row of bushes, then headed through a clump of woods before arriving at Geovanis's house.

"Where's Alicia?" Frank asked, staring at the

empty driveway. "Her moped's not here, and we made definite plans to meet."

"Maybe she's at the police station," Joe said. "She told us she'd go there if there weren't any messages at the house." He frowned. "I hope everything's okay."

"Let's take a look," Frank said, hopping out of the Jeep and striding up to the front door.

Inside the house Frank and Joe found nothing unusual—just the slight messiness they'd noticed two days earlier. Frank glanced around for notes among the mail strewn on a side table, while Joe pressed the message button on the answering machine by the front window.

"Weird," Joe said, cocking his ear toward the machine. "The message tape has played all the way through, so no one can leave a message."

"That's bad," Frank said. "The kidnapper or Mr. Geovanis might have thought they'd left a message, but the machine didn't record it."

Joe glanced out the window, lost in thought. A prickle of fear ran down his spine. He didn't like it that Alicia wasn't here to meet them. Could something have happened to her while she was alone? he wondered.

Just then Joe caught sight of a small rowboat about a hundred feet offshore. Sitting in the middle was a man wearing a huge wide-brimmed straw hat and casting a fishing line.

A gust of wind blew the man's hat off, and as

the man struggled to catch it, Joe saw he was Jonah Ferrier. "Frank, look," Joe said, pointing out the window. "I wonder if Ferrier could be spying on the house. That stupid hat pulled down low on his face makes him seem pretty suspicious."

"How did he get here so fast from the Jared Coffin House?" Frank asked.

"I'm going to ask Ferrier a few questions," Joe said. "Even if I have to swim out to him. Luckily, I put on my bathing suit under my clothes this morning." He grinned. "Just in case."

"Not so fast," Frank said cautiously. "Ferrier may have a weapon or something. Maybe I'd better come, too."

"Don't worry, Frank. That guy's no match for me. Also, one of us should stay up here in case Alicia comes back."

Frank nodded. "Okay, but I'll be watching you from here."

Joe stripped down to his bathing suit, then jogged toward the water. On the beach he noticed a sailboard—nothing more than a surfboard fitted with a sail—propped against a sand dune. Perfect, Joe thought. He hauled it to the water, then guided it beyond the breaking waves.

Though the surf was much calmer today, Joe had to concentrate hard to keep his balance while he climbed aboard. Finally he was up. Grasping the handle on the sail, he steadied the craft against the brisk wind as he glided out to sea. Squinting against the sunlight and the salt-water spray as he zoomed along, Joe couldn't see Ferrier's boat anywhere.

Suddenly Joe heard a ripping sound. Glancing up, he saw the sail hanging in shreds above his head. Before Joe could react, the sail started to swing around wildly, and he knew he was in big trouble. He clung to the handle, struggling to keep his balance.

Joe held his breath as the sail tipped toward the ocean, smacking him into a wave. As Joe plunged into the water, the current swept the sailboard out of reach.

Joe began to swim for shore, but the current was strong. The harder he swam, the farther away from shore he seemed to go.

Panic welled up inside him. I'm caught in a riptide, he realized—and the fast current is sending me out to sea. I've got to get out of here fast—or I'll drown!

9 Bogged Down in Danger

Joe's arms felt like jelly. Everywhere he looked, he saw swells of water that were tossing him around like a cork. He opened his mouth for air, only to gulp down a load of sea water.

Joe tried to remember something he'd heard about riptides—swimming against the current is a losing battle, but swimming across the current might work.

Using the sidestroke, Joe swam across the current. After a few feet the ocean suddenly felt still. The riptide's gone, Joe thought. But I'm still not home free.

Catching sight of the shoreline on the horizon, Joe knew he must be three-quarters of a mile from shore.

A dark speck on the water was weaving toward him from shore. Joe waved wildly, hoping it was Frank. After a moment the speck grew larger, and Joe was able to make out his brother at the rudder of a small sailboat. Yes! Joe thought, letting out a whoop of delight—he'd had a feeling Frank would come to the rescue.

Frank brought the sailboat close to Joe and helped his brother in. Then Frank let out the sail, and the brothers sped back to shore.

"What happened?" Frank asked as he tacked the boat. "I saw you one moment, and you were gone the next."

Joe told Frank about the torn sailboard and the riptide. "I wonder if Ferrier could have sabotaged the sailboard, then planted himself in that boat to lure you out to sea," Frank said.

"I don't remember noticing anything wrong with the sail before I started out," Joe said. "But who knows—it may have been tampered with. Or maybe it was frayed and just tore on its own. I wonder where it went?"

Shielding his eyes with his hand, Joe scanned the water. The ocean glistened with sunlight, and all Joe could see was an expanse of blue-green water. The sailboard was nowhere in sight.

"I guess we'll never know what happened to it," Joe said. "By the way, did you see where Ferrier went?"

"I saw him row back to the beach in front of

the house next door, while you were busy getting the sailboard through the waves. I'm not sure what he did next, because at that point I was concentrating on you."

"Good thing," Joe said, grinning. "Now, where did you get this boat?"

"Luck," Frank answered. "A couple of kids had just come ashore to swim and have a picnic lunch. Since the surf's pretty calm today, they'd pulled their boat all the way up to shore. I told them you were in trouble and asked if I could borrow the boat for a few minutes."

As the Hardys approached the beach, Joe noticed a teenage boy and girl sitting on a towel. Frank waved, then carefully guided the boat into the shallow water and pulled up the keel. As the boat touched the sandy bottom, the Hardys hopped out and pulled it ashore.

"Thanks for letting my brother use your boat," Joe said. "I'd be halfway across the Atlantic by now without it."

"No problem," the boy said. "Glad we could help."

"Did you notice a man coming ashore in a rowboat?" Frank asked her.

"Yes," the girl said. "He pulled the boat onto the beach, and then he and a blond woman carried it up to the house next door. A few minutes later we heard a car drive away from there." She pointed to a gray shingled cottage down the beach, about a hundred yards from the Geovanises' house.

"We'll have to ask Alicia who lives there," Frank told Joe. Turning to the teenagers, he said, "Thanks a lot for your help." Then he and Joe walked up the path to the Geovanis house.

Once there, Joe took a quick shower and changed into dry clothes. Since Alicia still wasn't home, Frank and Joe decided it was time to question Harrison Cartwright. After looking up his address in the phone book, they walked out to the driveway.

As Joe climbed into the Jeep next to Frank, he said, "If Alicia's not here after we finish with Cartwright, let's go to the police."

"Good idea," Frank said, and turned on the motor. Suddenly he snapped to attention. "Wait, Joe. I hear something."

A crunching sound of wheels on gravel and sand came from around a bend in the driveway. After a moment, Alicia appeared on her moped.

"It's about time you showed up," Joe said as she pulled up. "We were beginning to worry about you."

"Did you go to the police?" Frank asked.

"I can't talk, guys," Alicia said abruptly. She climbed off her moped, flicking down the kick-stand with her foot. "I'm too busy now."

"You're *what?*" Joe said. He couldn't believe his ears. "How can you be too busy to find your father?"

Alicia walked over to the driver's side of the Jeep. "You guys need to leave," she said.

Frank looked at Alicia, his gaze unwavering. He could see the dark circles that rimmed her eyes. "Not before we find out where you were. We were supposed to meet here after you checked the house for messages."

Alicia's eyes flickered with annoyance. "It's none of your business where I've been," she snapped. "But if you must know, I went grocery shopping. Look!" Opening her backpack, she took out a box of spaghetti and held it out to Frank. "I remembered our meeting, but I had to go to the store first. I'm just too tired to talk now." She put the spaghetti back in her pack and started to walk away.

"Wait!" Joe shouted. He jumped out of the Jeep and caught up to her, then quickly told her about Ferrier and the torn sailboard. "Do you know if the sail was frayed?" he asked.

Alicia glanced down uncomfortably, tracing a pattern in the sand driveway with her sneaker. "Don't ask me," she finally said. "It was an old sail, so it must have just torn."

"Do you know the name of the blond woman next door?" he pressed.

"That's Katie Hall, the publisher of the *Island News*," Alicia answered.

"The person Ferrier was having lunch with," Joe said. "Are they friends?"

Alicia shrugged. "I see him over there sometimes on Saturdays dropping off magazines and stuff. That's probably why he was there. And now, I've really got to go."

"Alicia," Frank said, leaning out of the driver's seat. "Before you go, tell us whether you've heard from the kidnapper."

Alicia's head shot up, then she instantly looked away. "Please go away and leave me alone," she said icily.

"No," Joe said. "Your father's missing and you might be in danger yourself," he said. "Besides, we're supposed to be helping you, not deserting you. Come with us while we talk to Harrison Cartwright. We won't make you answer any more questions—Scout's honor," he added, flashing a lopsided grin.

Alicia's face turned red. "Please stop your investigation," she said. "The police are taking care of everything. I'm sure my father's fine."

"How do you know that?" Joe demanded. "And when did you go to the police?"

Instead of answering, Alicia turned and marched up the walkway to her front door. Looking back with a scowl, she walked inside and slammed the door behind her.

Frank and Joe exchanged glances. "Weird," Joe muttered as he climbed into the Jeep beside Frank.

"You're not kidding," Frank said, shaking his head. "But she didn't ask for her Jeep back. We can still investigate Cartwright."

"Yeah," Joe said. "But I'd like to know what's going on with Alicia. It's as if she's a completely different person."

The Hardys drove in silence to Harrison Cartwright's house, about fifteen minutes outside of town near a stretch of moors and a cranberry bog. The sun was setting, and patches of mist rose from the open fields of marshland and scrub.

A tall row of trees hid Cartwright's house from the road. As Frank scouted around for the driveway, a man wearing a navy jersey stepped out from the property and peered inside a mailbox.

"Hello," Frank said, stopping the Jeep. "We're looking for Harrison Cartwright."

The man crossed the road to their side. "Well, you've found him." Cartwright gazed at Frank from under the peak of a white yachting hat, his gray eyes twinkling. Cartwright's skin was weathered from the sun, and his hair at the edge of his hat was white, but he looked strong and healthy, his posture ramrod straight. As Cartwright shook hands with Frank, Frank noticed he was missing part of his little finger. "How can I help you boys?" Cartwright asked, smiling.

Frank told Cartwright that Geovanis had been missing since the dinner party the night before. "We wondered what you and Mr. Geovanis were talking about last night at the party," Frank said. "And did Mr. Geovanis mention anything about going anywhere after the party?"

Cartwright shook his head. "He didn't tell me about any plans. He was trying to get me to contribute money to the shipping museum, and I refused to pledge an exact amount. I told him it wasn't the time or place to fund-raise, and George got angry. I didn't see him after that conversation."

"What time was that?" Joe asked.

Cartwright furrowed his brow. "Oh, I'd say about eight—just after dinner."

"Thank you very much, sir," Frank said.

"You're welcome, and I hope you find Geovanis soon." Cartwright waved as Frank and Joe drove off.

"Now what?" Joe asked. "We didn't learn a thing from him. The trail's gone cold."

"Not really," Frank said. "We still need to track down our main suspect—Scarlatti. And also check out the museum again—see if we can find a link between the vandalism and Mr. Geovanis going AWOL."

About thirty yards past Cartwright's mailbox, the Hardys heard a pop, then a loud slap of rubber. The Jeep sagged to one side. "Oh, no,"

Frank groaned. "A flat." He brought the Jeep to a halt by the edge of a cranberry bog, and the Hardys got out.

As Joe inspected the tire, Frank glanced over at the cranberry bog. In the misty dusk he thought he saw something move. "Joe, look," he whispered.

As Joe snapped to attention, Frank made out a hunched-over figure in a dark shirt darting down a path through the bog about a hundred feet away. "I wonder if that's Cartwright," Frank said. "This guy's wearing a dark shirt, too, but I can't see much else in the mist. Why is he all hunched over—like he's sneaking somewhere?"

"There's only one way to find out," Joe said. "Let's follow him."

Frank and Joe jogged onto a narrow path that bordered the bog. Thick rows of cranberry bushes choked the swampy water, and the mist made the going treacherous. Frank kept his eyes on the ghostlike figure ahead, weaving its way through the fog.

Frank heard a sudden splash behind him, and he turned around to see his brother knee-deep in the bog. As Joe scrambled back to the path, his muddy sneakers made a squeaking sound. "I'm okay—let's just move," he said.

The Hardys continued down the path, but the figure was gone. "We've lost him," Frank said. "And the mist is getting thicker. Maybe we should come back tomorrow when we can see what's out here."

"Hey, Frank, what's this?" Joe bent down and picked up a small round object. Turning it over in his fingers, he said, "It's a gold cuff link shaped like an anchor, with the letters *EP* on it. I wonder if it belongs to the guy we were chasing."

Frank took the cuff link from Joe, peering at it in the semidarkness. Then he looked at Joe, his eyes wide with excitement. "EP—those are the initials of the *Ebony Pearl!*"

10 The Secret Tunnel

"What would the *Ebony Pearl* have to do with this?" Joe asked in surprise.

"Beats me," Frank said with a shrug. "Mr. Geovanis or someone could have owned some cuff links that came from the *Ebony Pearl*."

"Alicia told us her father was just a kid when the ship sank." Joe thought for a moment, then added, "Maybe he took them as a souvenir."

"Maybe," Frank agreed. "Mr. Geovanis could have been wearing them when he disappeared. It was a fancy dinner party, and he might have worn a dress shirt with cuff links."

"We'll have to show this to Alicia," Joe said, slipping the cuff link into his pocket. "If she ever talks to us again, that is."

Frank and Joe scanned the path for other clues, then headed for the Jeep. After changing the tire, they drove into town to pick up Callie at the newspaper. Soon they were all sitting down to a lobster dinner at the Easy Street Café at Steamboat Wharf.

"No way am I wearing one of these," Joe muttered, crumpling the plastic bib the waitress had brought. "I mean, I'm not two years old anymore."

Callie laughed as she and Frank put their own bibs aside on an extra chair. "A lot of people don't want to ruin their clothes eating messy lobster. That's why they give out these bibs. Still, I know what you mean, Joe."

"My sweatshirt can handle it," Frank commented. "It's seen worse."

Before ordering, Frank and Joe had filled Callie in on the case so far. "So, what are your theories about all this?" she asked as they all dug into their lobsters.

"I think that someone's looking for something in the museum," Frank said. "The culprit's trying to force Geovanis to tell him where it is, so he kidnapped him."

"What do you think the guy's looking for?" Callie asked.

"Who knows?" Frank answered, cracking open his lobster's shell with a nutcracker. "If we can figure that out, we might get more leads to Geovanis's whereabouts."

Callie took a sip of water. "What about suspects? I hope you've at least ruled out Mr. Ferrier."

"Not completely," Joe told her. "He was the only person who knew we were going to the mill. He had an alibi for the time we were there, but he could have an accomplice. And it was strange that he appeared in front of Alicia's house this afternoon."

Callie rolled her eyes. "He was dropping off stuff at the publisher's house—he often does that. He probably just decided to go fishing right then."

"Someone else could have heard us planning to go to the mill," Frank said. "And Ferrier's motive does seem far-fetched. Also, why would he ransack the museum?"

"I'm glad you're finally seeing my point of view," Callie said with a smile. "Now, what about Harrison Cartwright? There's evidence against him—his argument with Mr. Geovanis, then the shadowy figure in the cranberry bog near his property."

"But Cartwright wasn't wearing a dress shirt with cuff links when we saw him at the mailbox," Joe said.

Callie looked thoughtful. "Since none of your suspects has the initials *EP*, maybe *EP* does stand for *Ebony Pearl* and the cuff links belong to Alicia's father."

"I want to search the cranberry bog first thing tomorrow," Frank said. "I have a feeling the cuff link is a clue to where he is."

"I still think Scarlatti's our strongest suspect," Joe said, loudly cracking a lobster claw with his nutcracker. "He would have a key to the museum and know the alarm system. He wants Geovanis's job. And remember the secret passageway in his house that Alicia mentioned? If it's for real, it would be a great place to hide someone. Why don't we check out his house after dinner?"

"If we find nothing there," Frank said, "then we should go to the police. It's been twenty-four hours since Mr. Geovanis disappeared, and we can see whether Alicia's reported him missing. I also want to get into the museum again."

When Frank signaled to the waiter to bring the check, Callie said, "The strangest development in the case is Alicia's weird behavior. Why would she want you guys off the case? And what evidence does she have that her dad's okay?"

Joe shrugged. "I wonder if she sabotaged the sailboard—to scare us away. She knew we were coming over to the house. She could have planted the sailboard by the beach, knowing that one of us might take it out while we were waiting for her to come home."

"No way, Joe," Callie said hotly, her eyes

flashing with annoyance. "Alicia would never hurt anyone. That theory's even crazier than suspecting Mr. Ferrier of kidnapping."

"Maybe," Joe agreed. "But you must admit that Alicia knows more than she's telling. What if her dad stole something from the museum and then disappeared to make it look like he was kidnapped?"

Frank looked at Joe with curiosity. "And Alicia's helping him?" he asked.

"Either she's helping him, or she found out about his crime and doesn't want to turn her own father in."

"You guys," Callie said, pushing back her chair. "Let's get out of here. That lobster's made you crazy."

"Just the opposite," Frank said with a grin. "Your theory's pretty sharp, Joe. I wish I'd thought of it myself."

"Thanks, Frank," Joe said, taking the check from the waiter. "All in a day's work."

"Looks like no one's home," Joe said from the sidewalk outside Roberto Scarlatti's house. "There's only one small light in the downstairs hall."

"Good," Frank said as he scanned the mansion. He led the way up the porch stairs and tested the door. "Still locked," he muttered.

"Let's see if we can find an open window some-where."

Frank, Joe, and Callie explored the wrap-around porch. "Here's an open window with a screen," Frank said from the side of the house. "Let's see if I can pry it open."

Using the flat edge of his pocketknife, Frank was able to lift the screen, and he, Joe, and Callie crawled inside. Overstuffed living room furni-ture, faintly lit by the hall light, loomed up around them.

"I sure hope no one's home," Callie whis-pered, taking a few steps toward the hall. "Whoa!" An unearthly howl pierced the silence as Callie stumbled. Frank reached to help Callie, his heart hammering in his chest.

"I think it was a cat," Callie said with a nervous laugh. "I felt something soft brush against my legs as I tripped."

A muffled thump came from the hallway, fol-lowed by a louder bang. "That's no cat," Joe whispered, moving quietly toward the sound.

"It's coming from under the stairs," Frank said as he followed Joe. "But I don't see a closet door there."

"I'll bet it's Scarlatti's secret passageway," Joe said excitedly. "And Mr. Geovanis is stashed in there."

"If it is a secret passageway, there must be a

button or a spring somewhere that opens it," Callie said. "Let's see if we can find it."

Callie ran her fingers over the molding under the stairs while Frank and Joe pressed the panels along the side of the stairs.

"I think I've got it!" Callie exclaimed. Her finger rested on a piece of molding just above her head. "There's a tiny button hidden here." Callie pressed it, and a panel sprung open under the stairs. A faint moan came from inside.

It's got to be Mr. Geovanis, Joe thought. He peered inside, then gasped in amazement as someone fell into his arms.

11 Blown to Bits

"Alicia! What are you doing here?" Joe cried.

"I'm so glad you guys found me," Alicia said as she pulled away from Joe. "I would have been trapped in there all night with that lunatic Scarlatti around."

"Did he lock you in there?" Callie asked.

"No," Alicia said. "The door shut on me by mistake. I was—"

"What's that sound?" Frank cut in. They all held their breath, listening. A pounding came from the front porch, as if someone was climbing the stairs. Then a key rattled in the door, and the lock snapped open. "Scarlatti's home!" Frank said. "Hide, or he'll catch us."

The Hardys, Callie, and Alicia scrambled into

the secret closet and shut the door. It was dark, except for a faint thread of light under the door.

"Let's wait here for a moment to see what Scarlatti will do," Joe said.

"Shhh," Callie whispered. "He'll hear us."

Nobody breathed as Scarlatti moved around in the downstairs hallway. After a minute he thumped upstairs, causing the staircase to shake around them. Soon the distant sound of a TV or radio filled the silent house.

"Let's hope he's upstairs for the night," Joe whispered. "Should we try to sneak out through the living room window?" He felt around the panel for a button or spring. "Strange," he said. "I can't find a way to open this door."

"I couldn't, either," Alicia said. "That's why I banged when I heard Callie scream. I hoped you'd hear me and let me out."

"Well, your wish came true—for a moment, that is," Joe muttered.

"So we're stuck here till someone frees us?" Callie said anxiously.

"Remember the secret passageway I mentioned when we came here to look for Roberto this morning?" Alicia said. "I wonder if it leads from this closet. After all, the door was secret, and we had to find a hidden button."

"There's no passageway that I can find," Joe said, his voice muffled as he searched the back of the closet. "All I can feel is a wall."

"What are you doing here anyway, Alicia?" Frank asked. "Why were you inside the closet?"

"I was just about to tell you when Roberto came in," Alicia said, her voice a hoarse whisper. "I'm really scared, you guys, and at this point I don't know where to turn."

"Do you know where your father is?" Frank asked.

"No. But when I got home this afternoon, I found a note in our mailbox. The note was from the kidnapper."

"What did it say?" Joe asked. He'd given up searching for the passageway and was standing between Callie and Frank.

"It said that if I want my father back, I have to pick up a manuscript from his safe-deposit box on Monday morning and leave it in a trash can on the wharf when the ten o'clock ferry docks. But if I talk to the police or to you guys about this, Dad will die."

Callie caught her breath. "So your father's still alive! We have one more day to find him until you have to deliver the manuscript."

"Do you know anything about the manuscript?" Frank asked. "Why would anyone want it?"

"I'm not sure," Alicia whispered. "I only know Dad's working on a book about shipwrecks."

"I wonder if that's what the thief was looking for in the museum?" Frank said. "He could have stolen a few shipwreck artifacts to make the job look like a burglary."

"True," Joe said. "He could have pulled down the papers on the shelves looking for the hard copy of the manuscript, then turned on the computer to see if he could find it there."

"Do you have a key to the safe-deposit box?" Frank asked Alicia.

"The kidnapper included Dad's key in the envelope with the note," Alicia explained. "Dad must have had all his keys together on a chain when he was kidnapped."

"The kidnapper couldn't go into the safe-deposit box himself because he'd be recognized," Joe whispered.

"So the kidnapper wants my dad to give up what he's been working on so hard," Alicia said hotly. "I'm sure the kidnapper wants to claim it for himself."

"Shhh," Callie said. "Keep your voice down."

"Roberto must be the culprit," Alicia whispered. "He's jealous of Dad, and he knows the alarm code at the museum. That's why I'm here. I decided to sneak in to see if Dad was hidden in the secret passageway, since Roberto had mentioned that he'd built one."

"But where's the passageway?" Joe asked. "Maybe he just meant this closet."

"Maybe," Alicia said, sounding disappointed.

"I found the button to open the panel from the outside, but I couldn't find any button or passageway once I was inside."

Frank backed up to give himself more room. He thought the closet was getting pretty stuffy. As he stepped against the back wall, he felt something give way under his shoe—like a button being pressed, he thought.

At that moment Frank felt the wall shake. He caught his breath, his senses on alert. He couldn't believe it, but the wall actually started to slide open behind him.

"Hey, guys," he whispered, poking his hand through the empty space where the wall had been. "I think we've found our passageway."

"Are you sure?" Alicia said.

"Let's check it out." With his fingers brushing the walls, Frank stepped into a musty dark tunnel that seemed about two feet wide. He felt his way for ten paces or so, then the tunnel turned a corner to the left. Still feeling along the walls, Frank suddenly stepped into thin air with one foot.

"Whoa!" he cried as he struggled to keep his balance. "Stop, everybody. The floor's gone." Frank bent down and felt the hole with his hand. About six inches down, he touched a step. "C'mon, guys—there are stairs here."

Frank began the treacherous descent down the

dark stairway, not knowing where it would lead. "Let's hope these stairs aren't sabotaged, like at the Corn Mill," he said.

"Stop, Frank," Callie whispered. "This is scary enough as it is. Don't remind us of sabotage."

The stairs leveled off into another corridor—this one with a slippery dirt floor and dank air smelling of mildew. As Frank moved forward, cobwebs brushed against his face and something—he guessed it was just a spider—scuttled down his neck.

"I kind of hope your dad isn't in here, Alicia," Joe said from the back of the line. "This place is more like a prison than a basement."

"What's that?" Callie asked. Everyone paused, listening to a scratching noise at the back of the tunnel.

"I hope it's not Roberto behind us," Alicia said.

"It's probably a rat," Frank whispered as he heard a high-pitched squeak. "But let's not wait around to find out. Here are more stairs—going up this time." He started up a steep flight of dirt stairs.

"Yuck, Frank," Callie said, making a spitting sound. "You just gave me a mouthful of dirt."

"Sorry," Frank said. He bumped his head on something flat and hard above him. What in the world? he thought—I hope this isn't a dead end. Pushing up hard with the palm of his hand, he felt the obstruction give way. "Hold on a second, guys," he announced with excitement. "It's a trapdoor."

Frank pushed the door up and open, then poked his head out. A blast of cool night air greeted him. Clouds covered the moon, but Frank saw that they were under the gazebo in Scarlatti's backyard. A light was on in the house—Scarlatti's upstairs bedroom, Frank guessed.

Frank climbed out, followed by Callie, Alicia, and Joe. In the dim light cast by the house, Frank could just make out their faces streaked with dirt and cobwebs.

"Even though we didn't find Dad, I'm still considering Roberto our number-one suspect," Alicia declared.

"That reminds me," Joe said. He reached into his pocket, took out the cuff link, and handed it to Alicia. "Could this cuff link be your dad's?"

"I don't recognize it," Alicia said, peering at it closely. "It looks like an anchor, but I can barely see it in the dark."

"It has the initials *EP* on it," Joe said, taking the cuff link from Alicia. He told Alicia about finding it in the cranberry bog while they were chasing the mystery man.

"I'm pretty sure Dad was wearing a shirt with regular button cuffs the night he disappeared," Alicia said. "I don't think he even has any shirts that need cuff links. Could it belong to the kid-napper?"

Joe shrugged. "I'd like to ask Scarlatti about it. Even though it's late, he shouldn't mind answering questions that might help us find a missing person." Joe grinned. "*If* he's innocent, that is."

"We'll wait for you in the Jeep," Frank said. "Four people at his door at this hour would be enough to make anyone clam up."

"I'll bet it's going to rain," Alicia commented, glancing toward the sky. "I'll put the top on the Jeep."

Five minutes later Joe approached the Jeep, shaking his head. "That was a bust," he announced as he hopped into the front seat next to Frank. "Scarlatti wasn't too happy to see me, especially when I told him I was investigating Mr. Geovanis's disappearance. He said he hasn't seen Mr. Geovanis since their argument at the museum, but he's sure Mr. Geovanis is fine. He was just about to close the door in my face when I showed him the cuff link."

"What did he do then?" Frank asked.

"He told me he'd never seen it before. He said it was the kind of cuff link a ship's officer might wear for a formal party, and he thought *EP* probably does stand for the *Ebony Pearl*."

"A ship's officer?" Frank said. He thought for a moment, then added, "I'd like to search that cranberry bog again—even if we have to go there tonight. Mr. Geovanis needs help, and it can't wait until tomorrow."

"I have an idea," Alicia said. "A friend of mine named Bud Cortez works the night shift at the airport. He's a helicopter pilot. He might be willing to take us up in his helicopter and turn on the searchlight. That would be faster and safer than searching on the ground."

"Count me out, please," Callie murmured as rain suddenly spattered the Jeep's windshield. A gust of wind whipped the branches of a maple tree in Scarlatti's yard, while the bushes beside his front porch tossed around in a frenzy. "It's not a great night for helicopters," she added.

"Okay, Callie," Alicia said, "we'll drop you at home. But you really don't need to worry. Bud's a pro."

It was past ten when Frank, Joe, and Alicia followed Bud Cortez onto the tarmac at the airport. By now it was raining hard. Joe heard ominous rumbles of thunder in the distance.

"It's okay to fly a helicopter in this weather, but I usually don't recommend going out unless it's a real emergency," Bud said. He was a slight, dark-haired man in his early twenties. "And I think this qualifies as an emergency," he added, glancing at Alicia.

Joe climbed into the front seat next to Bud, then Frank and Alicia got into the rear seats. Bud flicked some switches on the instrument panel while the others buckled themselves in tightly. The rotor blades started to whirr, making a chopping sound. The helicopter rocked for a moment on the tarmac, then lifted off the ground toward the roiling storm clouds.

"I'll keep this baby away from those clouds," Bud said reassuringly as they chopped through the stormy sky. "I like to provide you with every comfort." As he spoke, a gust of wind shook the helicopter, and rain slanted down on the windshield. Joe could still see the lights of the island twinkling below them.

"How will the visibility be when we turn on the searchlight?" Joe asked.

"Fine," Bud said. "Helicopters can keep pretty low, so our view shouldn't be obscured by clouds. As long as it doesn't start raining any harder, we'll be okay."

Soon the helicopter was hovering over the cranberry bog the Hardys had visited earlier. "The Cartwright house is across the road to the left," Bud announced. Glancing out Bud's window, Joe saw a huge gray-shingled house on a bluff overlooking the harbor. Bud flicked on the searchlight, and a blinding stream of light poured from the base of the helicopter, lighting up the ground. "I'm going to search the bog and the nearby trees," Bud explained.

Joe studied the landscape below, scouting for signs of a shack or shed of some kind where Mr. Geovanis could be.

"I don't see anything down there, guys," Bud said, shaking his head. "But let's check out the trees on the eastern side of the bog."

A splash of rain hit the windshield hard. The helicopter bumped wildly in the wind, tilting dangerously to one side. Joe's heart pounded.

Bud grunted as he pressed the tail rotor, trying to bring the chopper under control. "Got it!" he cried.

A bolt of lightning streaked in front of them. "That's too close," Bud said as a deafening clap of thunder filled their ears. "It's wild out here. I'm taking us back. We can check out that stand of trees tomorrow."

Joe held his breath as the helicopter veered back over the moors, jolting through air pockets. This is way too bumpy even for me, Joe thought, gripping his armrests.

"I'm going to take a slight detour and circle around over the ocean," Bud announced, "so we won't be landing against the wind."

In a few minutes they were over the ocean. The helicopter dipped in another gust of wind. "Aren't we a little close to the water?" Joe asked. "Another few feet and we'll be water skiing."

"Hey, Bud. What's that?" Frank shouted.

Whirling across the ocean, coming straight at them, was a huge watery funnel.

"Now, this is something I did not count on," Bud said. "It's a waterspout! In plain English, a waterspout is a tornado over water. We've got to get out of here—and fast."

12 Trespassers Beware

"Hang on!" Bud shouted. He stepped on the tail rotor hard and the helicopter veered right, away from the storm.

Just as Bud turned, the waterspout changed course, whirling directly at them. "It's coming again!" Frank yelled. Spray hit the helicopter like bullets as the storm came closer.

"No way!" Bud cried out. Once again he steered the helicopter hard to the right, heading toward land. "Now let's go. Engines—full throttle."

The engines roared as the helicopter flew over the coast as fast as Bud could make it go. Looking out the rear window, Frank saw the waterspout

105

make a ninety-degree turn about a hundred feet behind them. "Bud," he said with excitement, "it's heading back out to sea."

Bud let out a low whistle. "Thanks, Frank. I like that news. That's where it belongs."

As the helicopter flew back to the airport, rain continued to pelt the windshield, but, Joe noticed, the wind was letting up a bit.

"The worst of the storm is over," Bud announced. "Still, we shouldn't stay out any longer. It's pretty choppy, and the heavy rain limits the visibility."

"That's okay," Frank said. "We got a good look at the cranberry bog. It didn't seem as though anything was there."

"I wish we'd had time to search the trees to the east," Bud said. "That's worth a look tomorrow."

"On foot," Alicia said firmly. "I've had enough helicopter riding for now, thank you."

Back at the airport Bud brought the helicopter down for a smooth landing on the tarmac. After climbing out of the helicopter, the Hardys and Alicia thanked their brave pilot.

"Callie wanted us to let her know when we were back," Frank said once they were all back in the Jeep. "No matter how late."

"Callie said I could spend the night with her," Alicia said from the backseat. "I'm way too scared to spend the night at home alone."

Frank pulled the Jeep into a parking space across the street from Callie's apartment on Ash Street.

"Hey, guys!" Callie shouted, leaning out of her second-floor window. "Come on up for a soda. I want to hear about what you found."

"Just for a few minutes," Frank told her. "Then I've got to get some shut-eye."

Once upstairs, Frank, Joe, and Alicia filled Callie in about the helicopter ride. Callie's eyes widened as she heard the details of the waterspout. "I'm glad you guys are okay," she told them.

"You can say that again," Alicia said, settling herself into a chair. "I wish I could say the same for Dad." She paused, then added, "I wish I knew more about the manuscript he's writing. I'll bet there's some information in it that would give us a clue about what's going on. But I can't get into his safe-deposit box until Monday, when the bank opens."

Frank studied Alicia. "I think we should go to the police. Your father's been missing for a day, and the police could get the bank to open for us since it's an emergency."

"No way, guys," Alicia said, shaking her head. "The note from the kidnapper told me not to go to the police. I'm afraid for Dad's safety if I do. Remember, I'm not even supposed to be talking to you."

107

"Alicia," Joe said, "the police can do some secret investigating. The kidnapper wouldn't even know. It's silly not to get their help—the situation's pretty serious."

Alicia plunked down her soda can hard on the floor, spilling some drops on her hand. "No! You may be trying to help, but I don't want to endanger Dad. Please don't go to the police—at least not yet."

As Alicia began to wipe her hand with a napkin, Frank, Joe, and Callie all exchanged glances.

"Okay, Alicia," Joe said reluctantly. "We won't go to the police—yet."

Alicia looked at him, her eyes glowing with relief. "Thanks, Joe. I didn't mean to get so mad." Her eyes swept over her three friends. "I really do appreciate your help. All you guys."

Glancing at Alicia, Frank said, "I've been thinking. Your father disappeared right after he'd been quoted in the newspaper about the balloon from the *Ebony Pearl*, right? If *EP* on the cuff link stands for *Ebony Pearl*, I wonder what the connection is between the ship, the museum theft, and your father's disappearance. And, according to Scarlatti, the balloon is a hoax. If that's true, who made up the hoax—the kidnapper?"

"I don't know," Alicia wailed, throwing up her

hands. "Why would the kidnapper make up a hoax about the *Ebony Pearl?* Maybe it's just a coincidence Dad disappeared the day the newspaper article came out."

Joe paced the floor. "Maybe instead of stealing your father's manuscript and claiming it for himself, the kidnapper wants to prevent it from being published." He paused, taking a swig of soda. "Maybe there's something in it about the *Ebony Pearl* that the kidnapper wants to keep secret. Could something in the newspaper article have tipped him off?"

"Maybe," Frank said as he considered all the angles. "But we're jumping to conclusions here. We don't know for sure if the cuff link means anything or not. *EP* could just be someone's initials, after all. We ought to do some research first thing tomorrow morning. Then I'd like to search the clump of trees we missed tonight."

"Any one of our suspects could be hiding Mr. Geovanis near those trees," Joe said. "Ferrier's dune buggy and the torn sailboard are still unexplained, Scarlatti has a major motive, and the trees are near Cartwright's property."

"I took that sailboard down to the beach earlier today," Alicia admitted. "I noticed that the sail was pretty frayed. I'm sure it just tore on its own."

"If you guys need to do any research at the

109

Island News, let me know," Callie offered. "Even though tomorrow's Sunday, there'll be people in the office putting together Monday's paper."

"Thanks, Callie," Frank said as he and Joe headed for the door. "See you both tomorrow."

At nine o'clock the next morning, Joe was standing in the downstairs telephone nook at the Great White Whale, talking to Con Riley of the Bayport Police. Cradling the phone receiver between his shoulder and his ear, Joe held a pen in one hand and a notebook in the other.

"We're looking for background checks on three men, Con," Joe said. "Roberto Scarlatti, Harrison Cartwright, and Jonah Ferrier. Anything you have on them would be much appreciated."

"I'll see what I can do, Joe," Con said. "Expect a call back in about an hour."

"Thanks, Con," Joe said. "You're a real pal." Joe hung up, then turned to Frank. "Maybe we should call the dune buggy dealer while we're waiting to hear back from Con."

"Good idea. Ferrier's secretary told us the dealer's name: Freddie Applegate." Frank pulled out a phone book from a shelf under the phone and leafed through the listings for the letter *A.* "Here it is—home and business. Since it's Sunday, let's try his home number first."

Frank dialed Applegate's number. When Applegate answered, Frank introduced himself and told the dealer what he needed: the names of all the people who had bought blue dune buggies with red lobster insignias from him. After jotting down the information, Frank thanked Applegate and hung up.

"So, what's up?" Joe asked.

"Applegate said that he only painted four blue dune buggies with those lobster designs," Frank said. "He sold all of them—one to Jonah Ferrier and the other three to names I didn't recognize. Applegate also mentioned that the dune buggies could then have been sold secondhand, but he wouldn't have those records."

"We could try to chase the other three people down," Joe suggested.

"I'm getting tired of wild-goose chases," Frank said. "Let's head over to the *Island News* first. We might find some old clippings there about the *Ebony Pearl*. I have a nagging suspicion that the shipwreck somehow relates to the museum theft and the kidnapping, and if we can find more pieces of the puzzle—"

"We might be able to crack this case," Joe finished with a grin. "Come on—let's do it."

Ten minutes later the Hardys were sitting in the library at the *Island News*, thanks to a quick call from Callie to the librarian okaying their visit. Huddling over the microfiche machine, Frank and Joe reviewed articles about the *Ebony Pearl* that had appeared in the *Island News* forty years earlier.

"Man," Joe said, "look at this. It says that all of the ship's officers went down with the ship—the captain, plus the first and second mates, and the purser—"

"That's the rule when a ship sinks," Frank cut in. "Passengers go first into the lifeboats. The captain is always the last to leave the ship."

"And here's a photo of the crew," Joe said. "The captain's name was Ross Harper," he read from the caption. "The first mate was Luis Rodriguez, the second mate was Henry Zukerman, and—Frank, listen to this—the purser's name was Carter Harris. He was twenty-three years old." Joe looked up from the paper. "Frank, does that name ring a bell?"

Frank sat up straight as he considered Joe's question. "Carter Harris," he said. "That sounds sort of like Harrison Cartwright, with the first and last names switched."

Frank leaned over the microfiche machine and studied the photograph. "If this man Carter Harris were alive today, he'd be in his early sixties—same age as what Cartwright would be."

"There's *got* to be a connection," Joe said with

mounting excitement. "I mean, this guy in the picture sort of looks like Cartwright—though it's hard to tell because forty years have gone by."

"Let's go back to the Great White Whale and wait for the background checks from Con," Frank said. "Then we'll head to Cartwright's. There might be a hideout on the property we couldn't see from the air. Plus, there's the eastern edge of the cranberry bog still to search."

"Good plan," Joe said, pushing back his chair. "Let's move."

Back at the Great White Whale, Frank and Joe were walking through the front door when they heard the telephone ringing. Frank sprinted across the lobby and lunged for the receiver. "Hi, Con, thanks for getting back to us," he said, catching his breath.

Frank was silent for a full minute, scribbling notes as he listened. "We owe you one, Con," Frank said, and hung up. Turning to Joe, Frank recapped what he had just heard. "Con told me that Harrison Cartwright bought a house on Nantucket thirty years ago, so we know he's been here for that long. But there's no record of his background before that—where he lived, or anything."

"Interesting," Joe said. "Maybe Cartwright *is* Harris. After all, the cuff link was found near his property, and Scarlatti said it could have been a ship officer's. Maybe Mr. Geovanis pulled off Cartwright's cuff link while he was being abducted."

Frank looked thoughtful. "Cartwright has part of his little finger missing. That's the kind of thing that would make a real impression on a ten-year-old kid. Could Mr. Geovanis have recognized Harris after all these years?"

"And Harris didn't want to be recognized—so he kidnapped Mr. Geovanis?" Joe shrugged. "Sounds possible, but who knows?"

"I wish we could get into the museum and look around for Mr. Geovanis's manuscript," Frank said. "Alicia's right—I'll bet it would clue us in to what's going on. But remember, the police have closed up the museum."

"That's never stopped us." Joe's blue eyes twinkled. "Let's get in later."

"If we don't find answers at Cartwright's, maybe we'll have to. Though odds are the thief stole the hard copy of the manuscript from the shelves and deleted it from the computer. I don't remember seeing any manuscripts in all that mess—just papers and files."

Joe chewed his lip as he thought. "What about the other suspects, Frank? Did Con tell you anything about them?"

"They're just your typical hardworking tax-paying citizens—nothing special in their backgrounds, no police records. Scarlatti and Ferrier are under forty, so they're too young to have been on the *Ebony Pearl*. There's no obvious connection between them and the ship. But they're still not off the hook—Mr. Geovanis's disappearance may have nothing to do with the ship."

"Let's head over to Cartwright's," Joe said. "We need to ask him a few more questions. But first give a call to Alicia—we have to borrow her Jeep."

"Good thinking," Frank said, picking up the phone. "We've learned the hard way that mopeds are no match for a dune buggy."

Half an hour later Frank and Joe were in Alicia's Jeep, heading toward Cartwright's place in a thickening fog. The thunderstorms had finally blown out to sea, and the morning air was still and humid. The sky was a steel gray color, and blankets of mist shrouded the fields and sea.

"There's not much chance the sun will burn this fog off," Frank muttered, flicking on his headlights. "It's too thick."

He turned left into Cartwright's driveway, a narrow rutted road that ran between tangled masses of trees and vines. After driving about a quarter of a mile, Frank saw Cartwright's enormous house rising up on a bluff overlooking the water.

"Wow," Joe commented, taking in the house

and the Jaguar convertible pulled up by the front door. "Cartwright sure isn't hurting for cash."

"If Cartwright was in fact the ship's purser," Frank said, "then he would have been responsible for the passengers' valuables. He could have stolen jewels and money from the safe before the ship went down."

"And lived off his ill-gotten gains ever since," Joe said. "Using a new identity so no one would know."

"It does make sense. By the way, Alicia doesn't know why Cartwright's missing part of his finger—I asked her this morning," Frank said. He brought the Jeep to a stop next to the Jaguar. Then he and Joe climbed out and strode up to Cartwright's front door. Frank used the brass door knocker, then the brothers waited impatiently for an answer.

"Someone has to be home—there's a car here," Joe pointed out.

"But no one's coming to the door," Frank said, peering through a window.

"Let's head over to those trees by the eastern edge of the cranberry bog," Frank suggested. "The trees Bud couldn't get to."

Frank and Joe hopped into the Jeep and drove back down the long driveway. After parking the Jeep on the side of the main road, they stepped out and jogged down a dirt road that cut along the eastern side of the bog. Soon a narrow patch of trees and brush appeared about twenty feet ahead on the left. The trees were dense, their leaves dripping with moisture in the fog.

"I can't see too far," Joe said, "just the trees nearest me." Glancing around, he caught a glimpse of something dark and square to his left. "Frank, come here," he called. "I think I see a shed."

Joe heard a roaring noise, like someone revving the engine of a car. The sound was coming from a break in the trees. At that instant a blue dune buggy with a red lobster insignia zoomed out of the brush. A man wearing a black ski mask was at the wheel.

"Frank," Joe called, "look out!" His heart hammering, Joe raced for the Jeep, with Frank right behind him. "We're almost there," he called as he saw the main road before him.

But before the Hardys could reach the Jeep, the dune buggy roared up next to them, blocking their way. With a rush of fear Joe realized that the dune buggy was corralling them. Like a cowboy herding cattle, the man was driving them right back into the bog.

Joe knew their only hope for escape was for a car to come along the road at that instant, but there was nothing in sight. Running back down the rutted road, Joe stumbled on a loose rock.

With a sinking sensation, he realized that the dune buggy had stopped right next to him.

The man leaped out of the dune buggy and faced Joe squarely, blocking the path to the main road. Joe saw a glint of silver. The man had a knife, and he looked ready to use it!

13 Kidnapped!

Joe lunged at the man, jabbing him in the chest with his elbow. Stunned, the man reeled backward, knocked off balance. Joe lunged for the man and yanked off his ski mask. It was Harrison Cartwright.

In an instant Cartwright recovered. Springing up, he came at Joe with his knife. Joe scuttled behind the dune buggy, then landed Cartwright a surprise kick to the side.

Cartwright fell down, dropping his knife. But before Joe could kick it out of the way, Cartwright jumped up, pushing Joe off balance toward the bog.

This guy's in good shape, Joe thought, grimacing while he struggled to fight him off. Joe felt his left leg slipping down the side of the ditch toward the soupy water. He had to do something fast—if he fell into the bog, Cartwright could easily nail him.

Making a final effort, Joe dug a toehold in the dirt with his sneaker. Regaining his balance, he brought his leg back up and kicked his assailant, knocking him down. Then Joe heaved Cartwright into the bog.

Joe didn't wait around to hear the splash. "Frank!" he yelled, looking frantically down the dirt road. No answer.

Joe heard the squeal of tires, then something red flashed into view at the top of the rutted road. It was Frank at the wheel of the Jeep.

"Am I glad to see you!" Joe said as he vaulted over the passenger seat door. "I didn't know what happened. Are you okay?"

"That joker came at me with the buggy," Frank said. "I dodged it just in time, but I hit the ground hard. I'm okay, though."

"That joker happens to be Cartwright. I pulled off his mask. Then I pushed him into the bog."

Frank shot a glance at Joe. "It's just a matter of minutes then before he climbs *out* of the bog. And now that we know who he is, we'd better get out of here."

Gunning the engine, Frank drove down the

dirt road just as Cartwright, dripping wet, was dragging himself from the swampy water.

"We've got to get to that shed before Cartwright and see if Mr. Geovanis is there," Frank said. "Do you remember where it is, Joe?"

Joe peered into the fog, trying to make out the dark boxlike shape he'd seen behind the row of trees. But everything looked the same in the bleak misty landscape. "We're going too fast, Frank. Maybe we passed it."

Glancing back over his shoulder, Joe caught his breath. Harrison Cartwright was at the wheel of the dune buggy, and he was gaining on them fast.

"Oh, no," Joe said. "Cartwright looks like one angry dude. Why do I get the feeling he's not finished with us? Floor it, Frank, or he'll catch us."

Pressing the accelerator hard, Frank drove the Jeep full speed ahead. "I'd like to get help from the police," Frank said, "but there's no way I can turn around. I wonder where this road leads?"

"Alicia's cell phone!" Joe cried. "It's in the glove compartment. We can call for help."

"Nope," Frank said grimly. "She put the phone in her backpack when she first got the call from her dad. Remember—she said that she wanted a phone with her at every moment?"

The Hardys were silent for a minute, listening to the roar of the dune buggy some fifty feet behind them. "We must have passed that shed a while ago," Joe said. "There aren't any more trees on our left, and I don't see the bog, either."

Frank glanced around. Mist blanketed the land to either side. All Frank could see was his own Jeep, the dune buggy, and a short patch of road ahead. "We must be on the moors," Frank said.

"How much gas do you have?" Joe asked. "I wouldn't want to get stranded out here with just Mr. Charm behind us for company."

Frank glanced at the gas gauge. "It's half full. I think we're okay—as long as this road brings us back to civilization in the near future."

"Whoa," Joe said. "Look sharp, Frank."

Twenty feet ahead—as far as Frank could see in the fog—the road took a sudden turn to the left. "Hang on, Joe."

Slamming on the brakes, Frank felt the Jeep skid, and sand sprayed up around him. Moments later the Jeep careened around the turn. Looking through the rearview mirror, Frank saw the dune buggy take the turn, then zoom up within ten feet of the Jeep. "Unbelievable," Frank muttered. "This guy doesn't give up."

Frank gunned the engine, determined to keep far enough ahead of Cartwright to avoid being rammed. "We've got to be getting near something," he said. "Unless this is a dead end."

Frank drove the Jeep over a small ridge, entering an area where the fog wasn't as dense.

"Hey!" Joe exclaimed. "What's that?"

Two tiny pinpricks of light were crossing the road about fifty feet ahead. "They look like car headlights. We must be at a crossroads or something."

"The sky's lighter over there to the right—maybe we're near a town."

Barely slowing the Jeep at the crossroads, Frank made a sharp turn to the right. It took him an instant to realize that he'd turned onto a paved road. "Joe, a real road. It may actually take us somewhere—"

Frank stopped talking as he realized what was causing the brightness in the sky. Looming ahead on his left was a lighthouse, the beacon slicing through the fog like a knife.

"Wow," Joe said. "This has to be the Sankaty Lighthouse outside of 'Sconset. I noticed it on our bicycle map. I wonder if anyone's in there who could help us."

"I doubt it," Frank said. "The Coast Guard usually keeps lighthouses locked. But we're near the town—Cartwright wouldn't dare try anything with other people around."

Shooting another look through the rearview

mirror, Frank saw Cartwright behind them, now about twenty feet back.

"Frank, stop," Joe said. He pointed left. "It looks like there's a man walking toward the road. He's wearing a Coast Guard uniform."

"Hang on," Frank said. He put on the brakes, causing the Jeep to career to the left and bringing it to a stop by the side of the road.

Caught off guard by the surprise move, Cartwright zoomed down the road past the Hardys. Frank and Joe were out of the Jeep in seconds.

"Where did the guard go?" Joe asked, looking up and down the road as far as he could in the fog. "He's nowhere in sight."

Frank shrugged. "Maybe he went back to the lighthouse—let's check." Frank and Joe tore over a golf course green toward the lighthouse. When the Hardys reached the lighthouse door, they found it slightly ajar.

"If the guard's not inside, then he's probably coming right back," Joe said.

Frank pushed open the door and stepped inside. "Hello?" he called. There was no answer. Glancing up, Frank saw a spiral staircase. It must lead up to the beacon, he thought.

"Frank, look out!" Joe cried from just inside the door. "Cartwright's here."

Frank whipped around. Joe was trying to slam the door shut, but Cartwright had wedged his foot and shoulder in and was pushing hard. With a final shove, Cartwright managed to open the door wide enough to slide through. He was holding his knife.

"Upstairs!" Frank shouted to Joe. "The guard must be up there. He could radio for help."

The Hardys rushed up the spiral stairway. Toward the top, they paused for a moment, pulses racing from the steep climb. Then they continued on.

In the tiny room upstairs the huge beacon flashed through the fog, alerting ships to the nearby shore.

"The guard's not here," Frank said. "Now we're trapped."

"Maybe Cartwright won't make the climb— he *is* pretty old," Joe said, breathing hard.

Just then he heard Cartwright's heavy tread on the stairs. A moment later Cartwright appeared in the doorway, holding the knife. Hunched over, he took a second to catch his breath.

"He's in better shape than I thought," Joe whispered to Frank. "But if we can get the knife away from him, we can overpower him."

Cartwright straightened up. "Why were you boys snooping around my house today? I don't take kindly to trespassers."

"You mean you don't take kindly to us figuring out your little scheme, Mr. *Harris.*"

Cartwright fixed Frank with his steely gaze, his

eyes gleaming with hate. "The name's Cartwright."

"Tell that to George Geovanis, the guy you're holding prisoner on your property somewhere," Joe said.

"George Geovanis?" Cartwright said. "I don't know what you're talking about. I barely know the man. As I told you, George and I had that little discussion about fund-raising at the Ferriers' party, but I haven't seen him since."

Frank laughed. "You expect us to believe that? If that's true, then you have a pretty rude way of discouraging trespassers. Do you always attack them with knives—when they're on a public road next to your property?"

"You were at my house first," Cartwright spat out, "checking out my garage and my car."

Joe looked surprised. "If you saw us at your house, then how did you get to the cranberry bog before we did?"

Cartwright smirked. "So Frank and Joe Hardy don't know everything?" he said, his voice dripping with sarcasm. "What a surprise. Well, if you must know, I suspected you were casing my house ever since our encounter the day before. I told my housekeeper to call me on my cell phone if she saw anyone fitting your description sneaking around."

"So you chased us all over the moors in the fog just to tell us to get lost?" Frank scoffed. "Even though we weren't on your property at the time? What a lame story. You were onto us as early as yesterday morning, when you tried to run us off the road. I'll bet you got Mr. Geovanis to tell you we were detectives."

Cartwright stared at Frank and Joe, unfazed. "You were on back roads not far from my property, and, as I said, I don't take kindly to trespassers."

"If you use your knife on us here," Joe said, "you'll be murdering us in cold blood—on Coast Guard property."

"I'm not going to kill you," Cartwright said with a sneer. "You boys aren't worth doing jail time for. But if I find you on my property again . . ." He stopped, slashing his blade through the air. "Let's just say you've been warned." Keeping his eyes on Frank and Joe, he slowly backed down the stairs, his knife in front of him.

When the Hardys heard the downstairs door creak open, Frank turned to Joe. "We've got to find Mr. Geovanis. He must be somewhere on the bog—the cuff link is our clue. Cartwright wouldn't chase us down like that if he had nothing to hide."

"It's true," Joe said. "What better place to hide a guy than in that deserted shed?"

The Hardys rushed down the stairs, but just as they were pushing open the lighthouse door, they came face-to-face with the Coast Guard officer.

"Sorry, boys," the man said, "no tours today. The lighthouse is closed to the public. The only reason I'm here is to fix this lock." He held up a screwdriver, then pointed to the lock in the door. "I had to go into town to get the right kind of screws."

"We need your help. It's an emergency." Briefly Frank told the guard the location of the shed and that George Geovanis had been kidnapped. The guard looked shocked, but he agreed to radio for a police unit.

"This had better not be some kind of hoax," he muttered as he took his two-way radio out of his pocket.

Without wasting another second, Frank and Joe raced back across the golf course and hopped into the Jeep. As Frank jabbed the key into the ignition, he prayed that Cartwright hadn't sabotaged the car. To his relief, the Jeep started right up. The Coast Guard guy must have come along at just the right time, he guessed.

"Floor it, Frank," Joe said. "We don't have a second to lose."

Frank made a U-turn, then careened back up the road. Soon he and Joe were bouncing up the dirt road through the moors. At the edge of the cranberry bog, they began scanning the landscape. "There it is!" Joe cried, pointing

128

at a ramshackle shed set back in a grove of trees.

Frank slammed on the brakes, and he and Joe jumped out. At the shed Frank flung open the rotting door, then froze in horror. The shed was empty!

14 At Sea with a Shark

Frank whipped around toward Joe. "We're too late," he gasped. "Cartwright must have taken Mr. Geovanis. We didn't get here fast enough."

"Could we have been wrong about the shed?"

Stooping down, Frank picked up a small piece of rope and a rag from a corner. "I don't think so. Looks like he gagged him with this."

"I hope he hasn't killed him," Joe said.

Frank blew out his breath. "You and me both." He glanced up and down the road but saw nothing. "Cartwright knows the police are probably looking for Mr. Geovanis by now. My guess is he won't risk being on the open road with his captive. Let's head for Cartwright's house."

"The police would have to get a warrant to

search his house," Joe said, "and that takes time. Cartwright would have Mr. Geovanis alone for a few more hours."

"Yup—and that's all he'd need," Frank said grimly. Frank tossed the rope and rag back on the floor, then the Hardys rushed to the Jeep. Once inside, they peeled up the dirt road toward Cartwright's.

Halfway down the driveway, Frank parked the Jeep next to some sumac trees. "We've got to keep a low profile—Cartwright won't exactly be happy to see us."

"That's for sure," Joe said. The Hardys stepped out and moved stealthily toward the house, keeping close to the trees. Just as the woods gave over to a lawn, Joe pointed to the side of the driveway. The blue dune buggy was lying on its side, the front fender smashed. "Man, is that guy out of control, or what," Joe said. "Well at least we know he's around here somewhere."

"I just hope Mr. Geovanis is okay," Frank said. When they drew closer to the house, the Hardys saw a moped propped up on its kickstand. Frank frowned. "I wonder who that belongs to?"

Joe felt his stomach knot. "It looks an awful lot like Alicia's. I hope she didn't panic and decide to come here at the last minute."

A scream filled the air. The Hardys stiffened, every sense on alert. "It's coming from the front of the house," Frank said. "And it sounds like a girl. Come on."

Frank and Joe took off around the left side of the house, tearing up grass as they ran. The fog was still thick, but they could see the edge of the lawn, where it spilled down over a sandy bluff. Beyond that, the harbor was invisible under a blanket of gray.

Another scream rang through the stillness. "It's definitely Alicia," Joe said. Beads of sweat broke out on his forehead.

"Over the bluff!" Frank yelled, rushing to the edge of the lawn. A loud roar ripped through the air as Frank gazed down the hill. His mouth went dry. About ten feet off shore Cartwright was starting up a motorboat. Inside were George and Alicia Geovanis, tied up back to back.

"No!" Joe shouted at Frank's side. Alicia looked up as if she heard him, her eyes wide with terror. Then the boat disappeared into the fog.

"Joe, look," Frank said, pointing up the beach. Anchored to a dock about twenty feet away were two more speedboats. "One of those babies has our name on it."

In seconds Frank started up one of the speedboats while Joe unhitched it from the dock. A moment later they headed into the fog.

"This is even worse than the moors," Joe said from the prow. "At least we had a road to follow then. How will we ever find them?" He stared ahead, trying to make out the horizon, but the sea disappeared into a gray cottony void.

"We can follow in the wake of their boat," Frank said.

Looking down, Joe saw the long V-shaped trail left by Cartwright's propeller in the water. "Good thinking, Frank. We'll just pretend it's a road."

Frank revved the engine, and the boat sped along, bouncing through the waves. Soon Joe heard the roar of another boat ahead. "Cartwright," Frank said. He opened up the engine full throttle. "I can't catch him—he's going too fast. But at least I can keep up."

They zoomed along for what seemed like hours, when Joe noticed a light stabbing the sky to his left. "Is that the Sankaty Lighthouse?" he asked. "It's in the wrong place."

"It must be the Nantucket Lighthouse," Frank told him. "I'll bet we're going through the neck of the harbor, out into the Atlantic."

"Where's Cartwright going?" Joe muttered. "To Europe?" He glanced to either side. As the beam of light swooped through the mist, he could make out yachts and speedboats bobbing at their moorings. "Cartwright's the only bozo crazy enough to take a boat out in this weather."

"Or desperate enough," Frank added.

Past the lighthouse the water became choppier, and Joe felt his stomach lurch. Several minutes passed while the Hardys stared grimly into the curtain of fog ahead of them.

Suddenly the boat pitched. There was a loud crunching noise. "We've run aground!" Frank said, frantically trying to steer the boat off the shoals.

Joe leaned over the prow. He could see a brown oval shape under the surface of the water next to the boat. He was relieved not to see any holes in the hull. "It looks like we've hit a rock, Frank. I don't see any damage, but then I can't see the whole hull."

"Hope you're right, but just in case, let's put on these." Pulling out two life vests from under the stern, Frank tossed one to Joe.

Joe put on his vest, then sat impatiently in the prow. How would they ever save Alicia and her father now? he wondered. Even if they could get their boat out of the shoals, Cartwright's wake had already blended into the choppy ocean surface.

The sea was ominously quiet. Joe leaned over, pulling off his sneakers. He couldn't stand doing nothing for one more second. "I'm going into the water to try to push us off the rocks," he announced.

"Good," Frank said, looking at a rivulet of water streaming into the boat. "We've got a leak here after all." He picked up an empty coffee can from under his seat. "I'll bail, and you try to guide us off."

A low rumble broke the silence, growing louder by the moment. "It's a speedboat," Frank said. "We can signal for help."

The Hardys watched as a boat appeared out of the mist. Leaning over the side of their boat, Frank and Joe waved and shouted. As the boat grew closer, Joe grabbed Frank's arm, a shot of fear running through him. "It's Cartwright!" Joe exclaimed.

"Yeah, and he's alone," Frank said grimly.

Joe sat down. He felt as if he'd been mowed down by a truck. "That means he must have thrown them overboard."

Cartwright slowed his boat as he drew near the Hardys. "What happened here, boys? Get stuck on a rock? Amateurs like you shouldn't venture out in this fog." He laughed—an evil ringing sound. "I could come aboard and kill you right now, but I see you've sprung a leak. So I'll leave the dirty work to the sharks. I just saw one offshore."

"You creep!" Joe sputtered. "What have you done with Mr. Geovanis and Alicia?"

"I put them where you'll never reach them— my favorite picnic rock at low tide." As Joe punched the air in frustration, Cartwright added, "Of course, at high tide it's a bit wet for

135

picnicking, as George and Alicia will soon find out." With one final chuckle Cartwright zoomed off into the fog.

Joe gazed down at the water. The brown oval shape under the surface had disappeared. Joe frowned. "The tide's coming in, Frank. Alicia and her father will be shark bait."

Frank looked thoughtful. "This might be our only hope. If the tide's coming in, we might be able to get off the rocks. Let's go back to Plan A." Picking up the coffee tin again, he began to bail.

In seconds Joe was in the water, trying his best to push the boat off the rocks. The boat made a slight grinding sound as Joe dislodged it. "We're off!" he announced, climbing back in. "Now how do we find them?"

"I'll follow Cartwright's wake in the opposite direction from where he just went," Frank explained as he started up the boat. "It's fading, but I can still make it out."

Joe bailed while Frank steered. After several minutes Frank stopped the boat. "What's wrong?" Joe asked.

"I can't see the wake anymore."

Joe scanned the ocean surface, but it was no use. The wake was gone.

A bloodcurdling scream pierced the air, and a man's voice groaned, "No."

"It's Alicia and her dad," Frank said. "It sounds like they're in trouble."

"If we can get them to keep yelling, we'll be able to track them by sound," Joe suggested. But before Joe could call out to them, he heard another piercing scream. "Angle right to three o'clock," he urged. "They're not far."

Moments later Mr. Geovanis and Alicia hovered into sight, chest-deep in water, back to back. Their hands were under water—tied up, Joe guessed. The Hardys called out to them, but the prisoners' eyes were locked on something else. Joe froze as he followed their gaze.

Twenty feet away a sharp gray fin cut through the water. "Frank!" Joe shouted. "We don't have much time. It's a shark!"

15 Story of a Shipwreck

Joe's words rang out through the fog, and Mr. Geovanis and Alicia immediately turned toward the Hardys. "Frank, Joe," Alicia called.

"We're coming," Joe said.

"Be careful of the shoals!" Mr. Geovanis shouted. "They're all around." Looking down, Frank saw rocks under the surface of the water. He slowed down, trying to navigate the boat closer to Alicia and her father, but in a moment he heard the hull of the boat scrape a rock.

"Can't do it," he said, shaking his head. He glanced over at the fin weaving through the water, closing in on the prisoners. His face paled. "Joe, let's swim over. If we can cut their ropes free, maybe they could swim back to the boat. They're only about twenty feet away."

The Hardys stripped down to their shorts. "Hurry, guys!" Alicia cried. "The shark's getting closer." As she spoke, the fin glided through the water ten feet away.

Frank and Joe lowered themselves into the ocean. "Let's hope old Jaws there isn't hungry," Joe said, grinning nervously at Frank.

"I heard somewhere that if a shark attacks, you should punch it in the nose," Frank said.

"Let's just hope we don't have to test that theory," Joe said.

The Hardys took strong crawl strokes toward Alicia and her father. Halfway there, Frank raised his face from the water to scout out the fin. He froze in midstroke. The fin was close on his right, making a beeline for him. "Joe!" he yelled. "Look out—it's coming right for us!"

At the last second the fin veered away, but not before Frank caught sight of the creature's snub nose. "It's a dolphin," he cried, flooded with relief. "I can't believe we mistook it for a shark."

"Hurry, guys!" Alicia yelled. "The tide's up to my shoulders, and I can't last much longer with my hands and feet tied." A swell of water drowned out her words as she gulped down seawater.

Once again the Hardys focused on the rescue

mission. The choppy water lapped at Mr. Geovanis's chest, and he looked tired and pale. Another minute and he wouldn't have the strength to stay afloat. Frank and Joe reached them in a few quick strokes and started to untie their ropes.

"I don't think I can swim to the boat," Mr. Geovanis said weakly. His body sagged, and his face went under water for a moment. "Can you help me?" he choked, spitting out seawater.

Placing himself behind Mr. Geovanis, Frank cupped his hand under the older man's chin and pulled him through the water to the boat, while Joe and Alicia swam after them.

Once they were all safely in the boat, Joe went back to bailing while Frank started up the engine. "Don't you think we ought to stay here until the fog lifts?" Alicia said. "We won't know how to get back."

"The boat's leaking and the tide's coming in," Frank explained, "so I think we have to try to get back. The sky looks lighter over there—that's probably the lighthouse." Frank started the engine and moved off slowly, following the glow in the sky.

After several minutes Joe said, "I can't control this leak anymore. No matter how fast I bail, the water pours in even faster."

"You're right," Frank said anxiously, watching

the hull fill up with water. Joe searched for more life jackets, but there were only the two.

Alicia shouted, "Look, guys!" She pointed to the left. "Over there." Half hidden by the fog, a small speedboat rocked on the water about twenty feet away.

"Cartwright," Joe said. "But why is the boat empty?"

"I'll swim over and check it out," Frank said. "If it's still seaworthy, we can stay in it until the fog clears."

Geovanis moved toward Frank. "I'll take over the rudder from you," Mr. Geovanis said with a smile. "That much I *can* do. If you give me the thumbs-up sign, I'll bring the boat over. But promise me—be careful."

Frank promised, then plunged into the water. Doing the side stroke, he approached Cartwright's boat as silently as possible. Once there, he stood on a shallow rock and looked over the side of the boat. Other than a flashlight and a rope, the boat was empty. There were no signs of either Cartwright or a leak.

Lowering himself back into the water, Frank moved toward the prow. The boat must have run aground, he thought, peering under the hull, but where was Cartwright?

Frank felt something tug at his legs. What in the world? he wondered. That instant, he was yanked down, cracking his knees on an underwater rock. Flailing his arms, he tried to grab on to a rock, with no luck. Whatever was gripping his knees was pulling him under the water. The saltwater stung his eyes when he opened them.

He raised his head, trying to see what was going on. A man wearing an oxygen mask, flippers, and a diving mask was dragging him down to a crevice in the rocks. Frank recognized the man's gray hair, and adrenaline surged through his body.

Frank's lungs were bursting for air—they felt as if they were on fire. If he didn't do something immediately, he'd drown. Turning his body around, he clawed at Cartwright, but he was out of reach.

Out of the corner of his eye, Frank caught sight of Joe's wet blond head looming up in the water behind Cartwright. Joe grabbed Cartwright's oxygen tank and mask, pulling them off in one stroke. Then he punched Cartwright in the side of the head. Caught by surprise, Cartwright loosened his grip on Frank's legs. Frank shot to the surface, landing a kick to Cartwright's face.

Frank gulped deep breaths of air. As soon as his dizziness passed, he went back under to help Joe. But to his surprise, Cartwright was nowhere to be seen, and Joe was coming up for air.

"He got away," Joe sputtered, once the Hardys were both above water. Breathing hard, Joe went on, "He swam away from me, behind some rock, and when I followed him, he wasn't there. Then I had to come up for air."

Frank glanced around. Alicia and her father were bailing out the boat. Otherwise, the sea was ominously quiet. Had Cartwright escaped? Or was he stalking them in the fog? Frank had the uneasy feeling that Cartwright hadn't given up.

A dark form rose from the water. "Joe, watch your back!" Frank yelled. As he spoke, Cartwright raised his oxygen tank over Joe's head. Joe whipped around, shielding himself from the blow with his hands, while Frank punched Cartwright in the jaw. Cartwright flew back, then sagged into the water, disappearing under the surface.

"Quick, let's get in his boat," Joe said. "He might try to pull us under again." Frank and Joe clambered into the boat. "Where is he?" Joe asked, after several seconds had passed.

Frank heard a faint splash and a gurgling sound. In a muffled voice, Cartwright cried out for help. "Sounds like he's drowning," Frank said. "Somewhere out in the fog."

"It's coming from over there. Let's find him."

Frank grabbed the flashlight in the hull of the boat and turned it on, pointing it into the fog toward Cartwright's voice. "I can't see him," Frank said. "But I'll leave the flashlight on the prow so we can find our way back."

"Wait!" Alicia yelled from her boat. It tipped dangerously to the side. "We're just about to go under. We've got to get over to Cartwright."

"You find Cartwright, Frank, while I help these guys," Joe said, lowering himself off the side of the boat.

Frank followed Joe into the water, then moved toward Cartwright's voice. About five feet off the shoals, he spotted him in deeper water, panic-stricken. "Help me!" he gasped.

"You don't deserve this," Frank growled, swimming up behind Cartwright and cupping his chin with his hand in a livesaving grip. "But maybe you'd rather drown than admit who you really are to the world." Cartwright looked at Frank, his eyes glittering with hate, but he was too weak to respond.

Back at the boat Frank and Joe tied Cartwright's wrists and ankles and secured him to a seat with the rope.

"Let's wait here until the fog lifts," Geovanis said. "We'll be safer that way."

"We may have a while to wait," Joe said. "But that's okay. Frank and I have enough questions to fill a month's time on a desert island."

Frank looked at Cartwright gravely. "We know that you're really Carter Harris, the purser on the *Ebony Pearl.* Instead of going down with the rest of the crew, you jumped ship."

"In a lifeboat meant for passengers," George Geovanis added.

"Yes," Cartwright said with a sneer. "And I made my way to Boston, where I started a new life, with jewels I stole from the ship's safe. A few years later I moved to Nantucket so I could do more sailing."

"Coward!" Alicia cried. "You let everyone think you were a hero—that you'd gone down with the ship. Instead you let some other person drown."

Turning to Mr. Geovanis, Frank asked, "And you recognized him from the *Ebony Pearl?*"

"Yes," Mr. Geovanis replied, his eyes flashing. "I have strong memories of the *Ebony Pearl,* and especially of the nasty purser who sat at our table at dinner. And when I met Cartwright at a fund-raising party for the museum last week, he made a comment in the same snide tone he'd used onboard years ago. Then I noticed that Cartwright was missing part of his little finger, just like the purser. He used to tell stories about how he'd lost it repairing an outboard motor. I thought it had to be the same guy."

"Now what about the balloon?" Frank asked. "How does that figure into all this?"

Mr. Geovanis gave a small smile. "I'm afraid I have to take responsibility for the balloon. You see, I wasn't totally sure whether Cartwright *was*

145

Harris, so I made up the hoax using a real balloon I'd saved from the *Ebony Pearl*. I knew Callie was a reporter and that she was visiting Alicia at our beach. So when I came home for lunch, I planted the balloon nearby, hoping she'd find it and write a story about it. I was curious to see how Cartwright would react to news about the ship."

"Ha!" Cartwright spat out. "Well, you soon found out my reaction—and it was more than you bargained for. But what did you expect? I'm a prominent Nantucket citizen. I wouldn't let you expose me."

Mr. Geovanis stared at Cartwright in disbelief. "When I mentioned at Jonah's party that you looked like Harris, I hardly expected to be kidnapped. You were going to kill me, until I told you that the world would learn the truth anyway—my suspicions are all in the book I'm writing."

Joe turned to Cartwright. "You were the intruder at the museum. You went there to erase Mr. Geovanis's book from his computer."

Cartwright nodded. "And to destroy the manuscript. I made Geovanis give me his key and the alarm code by threatening to harm his lovely daughter if he didn't obey."

Alicia's eyes flashed with anger as she looked at Cartwright. "And then you wanted me to take Dad's other copy from his safe-deposit box."

"That was a bluff," Mr. Geovanis cut in.

146

"There's no other copy in the bank, but I was trying to buy time, and the bank wouldn't open until Monday. I hoped Frank and Joe might track me down by then—and I was right." He grinned at the Hardys. "I made a mistake telling Cartwright that you guys were detectives—I'm sorry. I was desperate, and I thought he'd back off if he knew you were after him."

"So you tried to scare us by running us off the road," Frank said to Cartwright.

Cartwright nodded proudly. "Then I lured you to the mill. I wanted to arrange some accidents for you."

"How thoughtful of you," Joe said. "And of course, the cuff link was yours."

"Yes," Cartwright said. "George ripped it off during a struggle on the way to the shed." He paused, then added dreamily, "I wore those cuff links sometimes, but I never thought anyone would link them to the *Ebony Pearl* so many years later."

Alicia turned to her father, putting her arm around him. "Dad, tell us how he kidnapped you from the party with all those other people around."

Mr. Geovanis's brown eyes looked pained. "We argued about whether or not he was Harris, and he suggested that we settle our argument in private. So we took a drive. Near the cranberry bog, he took out a knife and forced me out. After

147

a struggle, he tied my hands and put me in that ramshackle shed."

"Then he returned to the party, ate dessert, and gave a speech," Joe added with disgust.

"But how were you able to call my car phone, Dad?" Alicia asked.

"I escaped for a moment the next day when I asked Cartwright to change the ropes on my arms and legs because they hurt me. We struggled for a moment, and I knocked him down. I made a run for his dune buggy, hoping his keys were in it. They weren't, but his phone was. I called your cell phone after our answering machine at home cut me off. It took only a few seconds before Cartwright caught up to me and cut us off."

Frank glanced around. The fog was finally lifting, and he could see patches of blue in the sky. Looking at Cartwright, he narrowed his eyes. "It's time to go, Mr. Harris," he announced. "The police are waiting for you."

The next day, Monday, the skies above the island were clear and the air was hot. Frank, Joe, and Callie had joined Alicia and Geovanis for a swim at the beach in front of their house. As Frank spread his towel on the sand, Joe jogged over to him, carrying his surfboard.

"Hey, Frank, don't get too comfortable. We've got some waves to catch."

Frank looked at Callie and shrugged. Then grabbing his surfboard, he ran into the water alongside Joe. "Aren't we repeating ourselves here?" he asked as a huge wave crashed off shore.

Joe grinned. "Just stay off the beach, Frank. One mystery a trip is enough."